The Ordeal of Andy Dean

THE ORDEAL OF ANDY DEAN

Douglas Hirt

Thorndike Press • Chivers Press
Thorndike, Maine USA   Bath, Avon, England

This Large Print edition is published by Thorndike Press, USA and by Chivers Press, England.

Published in 1994 in the U.S. by arrangement with Doubleday, a division of Bantam Doubleday Dell Publishing Group, Inc.

Published in 1995 in the U.K. by arrangement with Doubleday, a division of Bantam, Doubleday Dell Publishing Group, Inc.

U.S. Hardcover 0-7862-0220-3 (Western Series Edition)
U.K. Hardcover 0-7451-2624-3 (Chivers Large Print)

The text of this Large Print edition is unabridged.
Other aspects of the book may vary from the original edition.

Set in 16 pt. News Plantin by Lynn Hathaway.

Printed in the United States on acid-free paper.

British Library Cataloguing in Publication Data available

Library of Congress Cataloging in Publication Data

Hirt, Douglas.
 The Ordeal of Andy Dean / Douglas Hirt.
  p. cm.
 ISBN 0-7862-0220-3 (alk. paper : lg. print)
 1. Bank robberies — Rocky Mountains — Fiction.
 2. Orphans — Rocky Mountains — Fiction. 3. Large type books. I. Title.
 [PS3558.I727O7 1994]
 813'.54—dc20   94-8002

For Rebecca Jan

One

Suddenly Ben Masters was thinking of Rita.

Why Rita after all these years?

This was not the time to be thinking of her, he warned himself.

Yet . . . why now? Why after most of ten years should he suddenly think of Rita?

He forced the memory to the back of his mind. At the moment, Ben Masters had more urgent matters to occupy his thoughts.

Scarcely aware of the perspiration that dampened his palms, Ben Masters brushed back his frock coat. He unhooked the hammer thong from his pistol and loosened it in the leather. As the black coat dropped back in place, he dragged a sticky hand across his chest and squinted into the morning sun. Its heat fell full and comfortable upon his nut brown face — a face carved and ravaged by sun and wind.

At thirty, Ben looked fifty, and he felt — well, at the moment he felt old and used up.

Farther up the street Neville Hallidae slouched against a porch upright and casually batted away a fly. Though hidden beneath a broad hat, Ben knew that Neville Hallidae's eyes were fixed upon the building across the street. Near the building's tall doors, Turner Wilson was bent over adjusting a strap on one of his spurs. When Wilson straightened up, his dirty duster parted briefly, revealing the worn handle of a bowie tucked under his holster belt.

Ben frowned.

Wilson never strayed far from that big knife. He'd not hesitate to employ its keen edge, given half an excuse.

Farther up the street Scott Mcintyre's heavy boots were clumping down the wooden sidewalk. He was seemingly in no great hurry to be anywhere . . . precisely as Neville Hallidae had instructed him to behave. Mcintyre was a big man, fully as tall as Ben himself, but wider and with heavy jowls that hung like excess baggage down the sides of his face. Mcintyre paid no attention to Turner Wilson as he passed him by and stepped through the heavy double doors of the bank.

Ben shifted his view in time to see the slight bob of Hallidae's hat. With a heavy breath that couldn't quite settle his nerves, Ben touched his own hat in reply. His hand paused a moment to clutch the red bandanna around his neck. He glanced toward the end of town, where Tom Deveraux straddled a bay gelding,

8

holding the reins of their four horses and the pack mule.

Shrugging off the lingering bit of anxiety, Ben Masters began his timed steps toward the bank.

"What will you do now, Mrs. Hamil . . . I mean, now that George is . . . ?" Malcolm Deeder cut his words short and his cheeks reddened. He glanced down at the withdrawal slip that Kathleen Hamil had pushed at him under the teller grate.

Kathleen Hamil had stiffened slightly at the mention of her husband's name. Even so, she was getting used to his being gone. Her own father had died young, leaving a widowed mother and three children. Secretly, Kathleen had harbored fears of being a widow woman herself, though she never imagined it would happen so soon. In some respects, she was more prepared for the tragedy when it finally did come than most women would have been.

At least I didn't have three children.

A glint of moisture came to her eyes as she thought of the children she would never have with George.

The bank teller stammered quickly, "I . . . I didn't mean to be indelicate, Mrs. Hamil."

Kathleen smiled. Smiling was becoming easier as the days passed. "It's all right, Mr.

Deeder. A woman has to get on with her life when she suddenly finds herself alone. At least George didn't leave me penniless." She smiled thinly. "He was a good provider."

Deeder began counting the money from the savings account Kathleen was closing out; all that she and George had managed to save, and some that George's father had left them when he'd died. Eighteen crisp hundred-dollar bills, a twenty, six ones, and some change. Deeder snapped the paper smartly through his fingers and laid the bills out so that all the edges precisely aligned, and all the faces stared in the same direction.

"There you have it. Eighteen hundred twenty-six dollars and forty-three cents. That's a tidy sum for a woman alone. You won't be keeping all this cash in that cabin of yours?" Deeder's eyebrow rose with genuine concern. A movement caught his eye as a man stepped through the front door.

"Oh, no," Kathleen answered. "My baggage is at this very moment being delivered to the depot. I am leaving Buena Vista on the two o'clock train this afternoon."

"Leaving? Where to, Mrs. Hamil?" Malcolm Deeder refocused his attention on the woman in the black dress on the other side of the iron grillwork. At twenty-five, Kathleen Hamil cut a fine figure. Her auburn hair was tied up in a proper bun at the back of her head. Beneath the black hat, brown eyes peered brightly at the bank teller. The swollen redness had faded from them in the three weeks since that morning when the timbers on the eighth level had given way and the cloud of dust bellowed from the mine's mouth. Seven bodies were finally recovered, but George's had not been among them. There had been nothing to bury but a symbolic empty box.

"Pitkin," she said. "My sister, Marie, and her husband have asked me to stay with them while I get my life back in order." Kathleen gathered up the money and methodically recounted the bills, even though she had tallied them as Deeder had laid them out.

"I'm sorry to hear you'll be going, Mrs. Hamil. You will be missed. Folks around here —"

A voice rang out at the front of the bank. Deeder, and a second teller behind the cage with him, looked up. Kathleen Hamil turned, her mouth forming a huge O; the money clasped in her fingers was momentarily forgotten.

"Hands up where I can see 'em," Neville Hallidae said, stepping through the open doorway. Ben Masters slipped in behind him, cast-

11

ing a backward glance into the empty street before shutting the tall doors to the bank behind Wilson.

The darkness inside cut a sharp edge against the bright morning, despite the twin shafts of sunlight slanting through the windows where dust motes swirled and flashed. A revolver tipped up into view from under Turner Wilson's slicker. Scott Mcintyre sidled up alongside one of the two tall windows and peered out at the dusty street. Neville Hallidae's footsteps made a hollow thump on the wooden floor. Kathleen Hamil's eyes leaped from the revolver in Hallidae's hand to the red bandanna hiding his face.

"Fill it up, bankman," he said, tossing a canvas sack over the top of the iron grill. The revolver waved at the cash drawer.

Deeder gave a quick, nervous nod of his head and began shoveling packets of new bills into the bag.

"You too, mister." Hallidae's pistol motioned at the second teller.

"Yes, sir." He dove into his cash drawer and came up with packets of crisp bills, freshly arrived from the mint in Denver.

Another mine payroll late this month, Ben mused.

A door in the back wall opened and a heavyset man Ben guessed to be around fifty stepped in from the office. "What's going on here — ?" His words caught like a fishbone in his throat. He sucked in a breath that took up the little slack in the heavy gold Dickens' chain girdling his paunch from vest pocket to vest pocket.

Ben moved up behind the startled man and nudged him with the barrel of his revolver. "We're making a little withdrawal," he said, his breath puffing out the bandanna.

By the window where Mcintyre was keeping a lookout, Ben heard a muffled chuckle. Ben relieved the startled man of the gold watch and heavy chain. He rummaged through the man's coat pockets and unburdened his wallet of its cash.

Hallidae glanced quickly around the bank, blinking at a rivulet of sweat that stung his eyes. "Sit him down over there," he said, words clipped short. To the tellers he snapped, "Hurry it up, damn it."

The canvas sack fattened.

Ben sat the rotund fellow in a straight-back chair.

Kathleen Hamil watched, not fully grasping the events whirling about her.

"What's that you got there?" Hallidae asked.

His question shocked her out of her trance. Instinctively, she clutched the money tighter to herself.

"Here, hand that over, lady."

Kathleen's head shook. She took a step backward as her brown eyes widened to match the gape of her mouth. Hallidae reached for the money. She took another step away and backed into Ben, who reached around from behind.

"Noooo!" she cried as Ben wrenched the bills from her hands. She spun around and kicked at his shin. He sidestepped and caught her arm as clawed fingers lashed out at him. She was a pretty thing, Ben noticed, and spunky too. He fought to pin her arms at her sides.

Turner Wilson laughed indecently from somewhere behind Ben. "Wrestle her to the floor so's we each can take a turn at her," he said.

Kathleen struck out again with a foot, and scratched his arms where they encircled her. "It's all I have!" she cried.

Ben tightened his grip about her arms.

Turner was leering openly now. "Let me have a feel too, Spyglass."

"Shut up!" Hallidae barked.

Kathleen got a hand free, caught a corner of Ben's bandanna, and yanked it off. A sudden hush settled over the bank and she stared full into his face.

Hallidae had warned them. He had said

14

more than once that if their faces were ever seen, they'd have to permanently shut the eyes that saw, or run the risk of being identified later.

Time seemed to slow, like cooling wax down the side of a candle. Ben's fist tightened around the revolver in his hand. He knew he had to do — what Neville expected him to do. Yet Ben had never killed except in self-defense.

Despite Neville's warnings, something inside Ben refused to bring the gun up and use it. He pushed Kathleen away and pulled the mask back up over his face, shoving her wadded-up bills into his coat pocket. He turned to meet the challenging look in Hallidae's eyes.

"Let's get out of here!" Ben said.

Hallidae nodded and took the sack from the teller. "In there, all of you," he said, waving the gun at the open vault. As they herded the people into the vault, Hallidae snagged Ben by the sleeve. "You got to do it, Ben."

"Leave her be."

Hallidae's dark eyes narrowed under the wide brim of his hat.

"I said leave her be." Ben pulled free of Hallidae's grasp and swung the vault door shut, scrambling the combination.

Neville Hallidae tugged down his mask. "I hope you know what the hell you've done,

Masters." The two men sized each other up. They had ridden together for three years, and both men knew what the other was capable of if push came to shove. Hallidae was the leader, Ben his second in command. Ben understood that Neville would not allow this insubordination to go by, yet here and now was not the time to work out their differences.

"Neville! Someone heading toward the bank," Mcintyre said from the window. His alarm sliced the tension like a hot knife through lard.

Neville held Ben in a tightening look a moment longer, then tucked the canvas money sack under his arm and signaled for the others to remove their masks and hide their weapons. "We'll talk about this later," Hallidae said, then glancing at each of them, he told them to act casual.

The man coming across the street was wearing a brown day coat, angling in the general direction of the bank when Hallidae and the others stepped out. As the man drew near, Neville averted his face.

Up the street Tom Deveraux sucked in a final lungful of smoke from his cigarette, bringing its glowing end dangerously close to the tips of his fingers. Deveraux flicked the cigarette away and tapped his heels. His horse plodded lazily forward, the four mounts and the mule that he held by the reins coming easily along.

They mounted up. Spiders inched along Ben's spine as they slowly rode away, but he resisted the urge to look back until they reached the edge of town. And when he finally did so, the man in the brown coat was back outside the bank, his hat in hand, scratching his head and looking their way.

Neville picked up the pace.

"What happened in there?" Tom asked as they bounded west toward the rising ground of the Collegiate Mountain Range that rimmed the wide valley where the town of Buena Vista lay. No one had said a word, and that was enough to arouse Deveraux's curiosity.

"Ain't none of your concern, Cotton," Turner Wilson said.

"It's as much his as any of ours," Ben said. He turned in his saddle. "I got careless. My face was seen."

Tom's brown lips puckered and he blew out a soulful whistle. "What'd you do about it, Ben? I didn't hear no shootin'."

"Old Spyglass turned chicken shit," Turner said with a grin. "He just let that lady look him in the face."

Ben came around. "We'd of had the whole town breathing down our necks if I fired a shot in there," he said, knowing full well that

17

was not the reason he had held his fire.

Turner's grin widened. The big bowie knife had suddenly appeared from under his slicker. "I could have done it real quiet," he said with an eager glint in his pale blue eyes.

"And you'd have enjoyed that, too," Ben said flatly.

"Certainly would have. But first I'd have seen to some personal business with her."

Ben Masters looked away from the smaller man.

Turner laughed aloud and shed his slicker in the growing heat of the morning.

Scott Mcintyre chuckled. "Aw, Turner, you wouldn't go and hurt a lady like that."

Turner's eyes bore down on Mcintyre.

"What do you know about anything, Fish Brain?"

Mcintyre's laugh went high and shaky, as if to say that he was really only joking.

They rode on in silence awhile after that. Finally, Tom said to no one in particular, "I for one am glad nobody got hurt. The truth of the matter is, when no blood is spilled, the law ain't near half as anxious to come after us."

Ben Masters grunted his agreement.

Neville Hallidae said nothing, but Ben caught the outlaw leader's glowering scowl.

The subject was a long way from being talked out.

Two

"Papa, here's something I fixed for you to keep you along the way," Andoreana Dean said, handing her father a basket covered with a checked cloth.

Franklin Dean dropped the cinch buckle and sleeved sweat from his brow. Still early morning, it was already warm; it would be another bacon fryer. He relished the thought, for in another month these mountains would be turning cold. Franklin Dean liked his days hot. Especially for traveling. The heat drew out the perfume of the pine trees — a welcome change from the coal oil and rock dust he was used to.

"Thank you, Andoreana," he said, peeking under a corner of the cloth. "You fixed this up all by yourself?"

Andoreana's shoulders rolled in a small shrug. "I helped Mama. I pressed out the dough, filled them, and pinched them. But Mama put them in the oven. She cut up the carrots, too."

Franklin grinned. "Well, someday you'll be cutting the carrots yourself," he said, giving his daughter a bear-size shoulder hug.

"I know. When I'm older," Andoreana said

with exaggerated patience, as if growing up was something to endure rather than relish. Andoreana twisted out of his grip and skipped back to the cabin. "Susie Meyers wants to say goodbye too," she called over her shoulder.

Franklin Dean couldn't contain a smile as he returned to the task of hitching the team. From the open door of the tool shed, Randy Dean stepped out into the sunshine dragging two eight-foot planks that weighed more than he did.

"Let me help you with those, son," Franklin said, dropping the straps again.

"These are the best I could find," the gangling boy said. At fifteen, Randy's arms seemed too long for his shirt sleeves, and his pants legs too short. His face was beginning to break out, and the bib of his overalls swallowed up his skinny chest. But there was budding strength there, Franklin knew. As a lad, he too had looked like a walking fence post, and it wasn't until he'd nearly reached twenty that muscle had caught up with bone, and onetime bullies began to steer a course around him.

"Figure they'll work, Pa?"

Franklin set each timber on the back edge of the wagon and stepped back to study the angle they made to the ground. He narrowed an eye at their thickness. He nodded his head and pretended not to notice the great smile that stretched the boy's face all out of shape. "I reckon they will work just fine, son. I'll find me a couple strong backs and we'll shove that fancy new stove up there and lash it in place. But when I get back it'll just be you and me, boy, and your ma, what will have to unload it."

"I can help, too," Andoreana said.

Franklin turned on his heels, surprised. "You walk like an Indian mouse, little lady."

Andoreana giggled. She liked it when her father called her that. It meant that she was truly a *lady,* and that someday she would be a big lady — like her mother — and, she hoped, married to a man just like her father. She said, "Susie Meyers wants to say goodbye," and held the doll out in both hands.

Franklin took the rag doll gently in his big hands and said, "Goodbye, Susie."

"Susie *Meyers,*" Andoreana corrected firmly. "She does not like to be called just Susie."

"Well, excuse me, Susie *Meyers,*" he said, grinning. "You take care of my Andoreana while I am away."

Andoreana reached up for the doll and hugged it to herself. "I will take care of Susie Meyers, Papa. She's too little to take care of me."

"Oh, I see."

21

Clarissa Dean came out of the house. She was wearing a brown cotton summer dress, and her red hair was tied up in a ribbon on the back of her head. In her fingers a scrap of paper fluttered in the breeze as she strode purposefully to the wagon. "Looks like you got yourself a lot of help, Franklin," she said, running her fingers through Andoreana's brushed hair.

"Sure do, Clara. This here is my sending-off party."

"Papa, why can't we all go together?" Andoreana said.

He went down on his haunches to bring his eyes level with hers. "Because we have chores to tend to here. There are the chickens and hogs to feed, and the gardens to water and weed. We can't let those chores go undone."

Andoreana frowned, but she knew that her father spoke the truth. "I'll miss you, Papa."

"We will all miss you," Clarissa added.

"It will only be a couple days. I'll be back before you know it."

Clarissa put the scrap of paper into his hand. Franklin looked at it even though she had shown it to him every evening since the decision had been made. It had been torn from a Granger's Supply House catalog that she'd found discarded alongside Mullier's General Store in Hays, Kansas, three years ago. She had kept the picture in her sewing box ever since, turning to gaze upon its white porcelain doors and shiny nickel-plated rods and corners shaped like seashells. It was only a simple line drawing, but her imagination filled in the colors.

"Now, I know you aren't going to find a Helmut & Schmidt stove just like this one." There was a bit of carefully placed disappointment in her voice. "But if you could find something that looks like it — well, it's just about perfect, Franklin. Be certain the oven is large enough for my baking, and that it has a bun warmer, and . . ." Here she paused and lifted her blue eyes with wide, shining sincerity. "And if you could find one that has a water heater, with a two-gallon holding tank . . ." She bit down on her lower lip and looked earnestly up at him.

Franklin folded the finger-worn paper into his shirt pocket. "Colorado Springs is the biggest place between here and Denver. I'll find you a stove with a three-gallon hot-water tank if I have to visit every store in the place!"

Her face broke out in a smile that outdid Randy's. She reached up and gave him a discreet kiss upon the cheek. There were the children around, after all.

Franklin finished hitching up the horses and climbed aboard the wagon.

"Be careful, Papa," Andoreana said, taking his big, rough fingers into her small, soft hands.

"I will, darling." He looked to his wife. "You take care of things here, Clara."

"We'll be all right," she said.

Franklin's expression turned worried. "Now you be aware of that old stove, Clara. Don't let it burn unattended. And keep a bucket of water handy. With that crack in the firebox, you just can't be too careful."

"I said we will be all right." Clarissa smiled.

"Papa, you gonna ask Jesus to be with you on your trip?"

"Why certainly," he said, giving her finger a squeeze. "You want to say it?"

Andoreana bowed her head, and the others did the same. "Dear Jesus, please be with Papa while he is gone away. Give him safety on the road, and don't let the wagon wheels squeak too much or run dry. Help him find Mama the stove she needs — and wintergreen sticks for Randy and me," she added as an afterthought. "And please bring him home safely to us. Amen."

"Thank you, Andoreana," Franklin said, giving his daughter a smile. "I'll be all right now."

Clarissa dropped an arm over Andoreana's shoulder and another around Randy's waist, and stepped back from the wagon.

"See you in about a week," Franklin said.

"You got the money?" Clarissa asked.

He patted his bulging pocket where the pouch of gold nuggets, gleaned from their small claim, resided bulkily. "Love you," he said and snapped the reins. The wagon rumbled away. Franklin looked back at his family waving him on his way. Then the narrow, rutted track took a turn and the trees closed in behind him.

Walter Devon swung off the tall horse and kicked at a pine bough that had been pressed into the soft earth near a seep. He spanned the hoofprint with his hand, then noticed a second hoofprint a few feet away — a smaller horse that carried a lighter man. Scanning the ground, Devon spied a glint of white in a clump of stiff, brown grass. He bent for it and straightened up, feeling a twinge in his back.

"What did you find there, Marshal?"

"Here's another one for your collection," Devon said, handing up the cigarette butt to the deputy. Landy fished into his shirt pocket and came out holding a second butt.

"They look like they could be from the same fellow."

Devon gave a short laugh and stepped into

25

his stirrup, swinging a leg over the saddle. He tried not to let the young deputies see the stiffness in his bones, and silently he cursed the aches that came with growing older. "You can bet the buttons off your Sunday best they're from the same fellow," he said, reaching back to his saddlebags for a handful of peanuts. He cracked a shell in his teeth and popped the insides into his mouth.

Stanley Hedstrom nudged his horse closer to examine the two paper remains in Landy's hands. "How can you tell that, Marshal?"

"Study them, deputy. What do you see?"

Stanley looked back. "I just see two cigarette butts, Marshal."

Devon cracked another peanut and spit the shell out. "They are both the same length, aren't they?"

Hedstrom looked back. "Well, yeah, I guess so."

"And the ends haven't been chewed, have they?"

Stanley scratched the back of his neck. "No, I guess they haven't."

"Some men chew their cigarettes, and other men just suck them. The fellow who smoked those doesn't chew, and he is a man who doesn't like to waste tobacco, either. He smokes 'em down to his fingertips before flicking them away. Now, some men value their fingers more than they value their tobacco. They end their smoke farther up."

Landy wrapped both butts into a scrap of paper and put them into his shirt pocket. Devon leaned forward in his saddle, chewing thoughtfully as he studied the ground around them. After a moment Devon said, "If I had to make a guess, I'd say the smoker in this crowd is the Negro, Deveraux. And if I had to guess some more, gentlemen, I'd say that Neville Hallidae and his boys are making their way to Buena Vista. Considering the lead they have on us, I'll lay you odds they are already there. Landy, let me see the map."

Landy Peterman fished the map from his saddlebags and handed it across to Devon. Unfolding the paper, Devon squinted, then pushed it out at arm's length. He grunted then and nodded his head. "Yep, lay your odds," he said as he refolded it and passed it back to Landy.

The deputies fidgeted and Devon knew they wished he would tell them all to climb down off their mounts and stretch their legs some, maybe even make camp for the night. But the old marshal pretended not to remember they had been in the saddle since six that morning. He touched the tall black horse with his spurs and headed slowly away.

By the angle of the sun, it was nearing six

o'clock. Twelve hours in the saddle, with only hardtack, jerky, peanuts, and half a canteen of water. But daylight meant miles to Devon, and that was all that mattered now, considering the lead Hallidae had on them. As Devon started up the rocky trail, he caught Landy's sideways glance at Hedstrom.

Stanley grinned back thinly and got his horse moving in line behind Devon.

Landy bit down on a piece of jerky and fell in behind them.

It had been a long day for all of them.

Three

"What happened back there, Masters?"

Ben glanced up from the fire. He finished pouring himself a cup of coffee. "You were there, Neville. You saw."

"I saw plain enough. And so did that woman. Damn it, Masters, sentimentality is a luxury we can't afford in our line of work. It ain't as if I never talked about this before. You knew what needed doing."

When Ben stood tall and straight, with a defiant arch to his back, he topped Neville Hallidae by two inches. "I didn't see that it was necessary, Neville," he said and strode to where his bedroll was spread out on the ground.

Hallidae's fists bunched at his sides. He glanced at Wilson, Mcintyre, and Deveraux. Ben had backed the outlaw leader up against a rock. Neville couldn't be made light of in front of these men and expect to keep their allegiance.

Hallidae came angrily across the ground and stood over him. "You got a beef with me, let's get it out in the open, Masters." Hallidae's fists tightened. His legs braced.

Ben was a rawboned, hard-hitting opponent, but Hallidae would have no choice except to take him on now. Ben knew it. So did the others. Hallidae had a reputation to think of.

"I don't want to fight you, Neville. Let's forget it."

"No, let's not forget it. I gave you instructions, straight and plain, and you went against them."

Ben heard the change in Hallidae's voice. Neville would happily end this with words instead of fists if that would save face.

Curiously, rather than thinking about this man who stood over him, Ben found his thoughts drifting back to the face of that woman in the bank . . . and to other faces as well. Faces he hadn't thought about in ten years. What did Rita look like now? Maybe she looked like that lady in the bank. For all he knew, that lady may have been Rita.

Ben stood abruptly and Neville braced himself. "It won't happen again, Neville. Tomorrow we'll ride out of here, and none of us will be any worse off than we are now."

The two men's eyes locked. Ben had conceded to Neville's authority in front of the others. He figured that was all Neville really wanted. Yet the victory had to be a hollow one from the reluctant nod of Hallidae's head.

"I'll let it go . . . this time," Neville said, easing back.

Ben carried his cup into the lengthening shadows beneath the pine and fir trees, feeling the chill of evening coming on. He followed a path to the edge of a valley and climbed a rock where the low sun shone full and warm at his back. It was a quiet place to sit and think. After a while he heard footsteps and smelled the smoke of Tom's cigarette.

"Come on up and sit," Ben said, gazing toward the valley below. Somewhere down there was the town of Buena Vista, but from up here only a misty evening purple could be seen filling the valley, and tucking it in for the night.

Tom climbed the outcropping and looked out over the valley. "Sure is a pretty sight." He eased himself onto a shelf of rock and stretched his long legs. His pants rose up on the scuffed brown boots where the laces had been patiently spliced a dozen times over. "Want a smoke?"

"No, thanks. Maybe later."

Tom shoved the fixings back into his pocket and took a pull at the stub of a cigarette pinched between his fingers. The sounds of the evening closed in around them. A buzzard hawk soared out over the valley, and they heard the distant chirping of the gray and

31

black juncos flittering in the branches of the piñon pine that clung to the mountainside below their rocky perch.

"What's troubling you, Ben?"

He looked over and said easily, "You think something's troubling me?"

Tom bent to tighten the laces on one of his boots. "I ain't never seen you and Neville go crosswise with each other like you done today."

Ben watched evening fill the valley below. "I couldn't see any good reason to hurt that woman, that's all."

"Neville's right, you know. They got paper out on you. I seen it. Probably got my picture posted somewhere, too. And Neville's as well. When you live like we do, you can't be too careful."

"Would you have killed her?"

Tom frowned and shrugged his wide shoulders. "I don't know. It ain't something I'd do happily. Not like Wilson would, anyway."

Ben tapped out the grounds from his tin cup on the rock, startling a nearby chipmunk to attention. "You have a sister, Tom?" he said.

Tom's lips came together in a frown. "No. Leastwise, not no more. I did have one once, but the Man in the big house went and sold her. Sold my mam with her, too. I reckoned after that I didn't have no sister no more."

Ben shook his head. "You know where she is?"

"No. I don't hear nothing about her or my mam since then. Pap was real broke up. Wasn't much a nigger could do about such things back then." Tom paused, then said, "The Man went and sold Pap sometime after that. I was ten or eleven at the time. I didn't never hear of him neither after that."

"Did you ever think of finding them?"

"Shoot, Ben, I wouldn't know where to begin to look. Besides, I wouldn't want them to know me now. Not the way I turned out. It'd disgrace them."

Ben felt a twitch in his cheek. "Do you ever think of her?"

"Who?"

"Your sister."

Tom pulled at his cigarette, let out a short yelp, and flicked the thing away. "I used to. But that was a long time ago. I was emancipated when I was fifteen. Afterward I believed that everything would be made right. Mam and Pap would be together, and Thelma would be with them. That was all dreaming. Ain't nothing changed. The nigger folk went back to work for the masters just like before the war, only this time they got to keep a little bit of their toil. But the Man in the big house, he still kept the papa bear share of it.

"I asked around some about them. No one knew where they were. I don't even know if they lived out the war. After a while of poking around and gettin' my ass in trouble, I decided to leave Georgia." Tom whistled and grinned. "I spent me many nights in a white man's jail. Seems like a nigger can't keep himself out of trouble in white man land. Moved west, gradual like. Jail to jail, more or less. I learned to fight real good. The fighting kept getting me in more jails. I reckon I'd have kept on that way 'cept I went and kilt me a white man. Figured I better skedaddle . . . ended up in Wyoming looking for work. That's when I fell in with Neville." Tom looked at Ben. "Why are you askin'?"

"I'm not sure." Ben tossed a stone that flushed a bird from a piñon tree. "This morning, before we hit the bank, I started thinking about my own sister. The last time I saw Rita, she was nine years old. She was standing on the porch with my folks, waving goodbye. I was twenty and going to make my fortune in the West. She'd be almost twenty now. Probably married with kids of her own. I started to wonder if my folks were still on the farm. They'd be in their fifties." Ben tossed another stone. "I don't know, Tom. Reckon there is some truth to the saying that when a man gets older he yearns to return to his roots?"

Tom laughed. "Not me. My roots are buried deep in white man's soil. I grow'd up on the water of a white man's whip, pruned so close to the stock I couldn't take my next breath without master sayin' it was all right. No, Ben. I have no wantin' to go back and visit my roots." Tom became serious then. "I didn't know you had a sister."

Ben grinned. "There are lots of things you don't know about me." He hefted a large rock in his left hand and flung it out underhanded. It made a slow arch in the air and started down, and as it did so, Ben hitched back his right arm and let go with a stone. Straight as a rifle shot, it smacked the larger falling rock before it had traced half the distance to the ground.

"You hit it, Ben!"

"It was a game we used to play, Joe Ratkin and Jimmy Singer, and me, when we were kids. We'd throw a boulder out over the edge of the palisade and see who could hit it first before it hit the river." Ben shook his head. "Funny. I haven't done that . . . or even thought about it much in twelve years."

"Bet you can't do it again."

Ben eyed the black man. "What you got?"

"Ain't got nothing. Nothing but a smoke

if'n you hit it again."

"You're on. You toss one out."

Tom fetched around and came up with a rock the size of a melon. "Ready?"

Ben nodded.

Tom swung back and heaved the chunk of granite. Ben eyed the falling target, hitched back, and let loose. The two pieces of rock clacked together and Tom shook his head, amazed. "I couldn't do that, not in a hundred years, Ben. Do it again."

But Ben had suddenly lost interest in the game. He said soberly, "I haven't seen Rita in ten years. For some reason I started thinking about her this morning. I don't know why. She'd be about as old now as that woman in the bank."

Ben sat a long moment, thinking. Then he said, "It's getting dark, let's get back." Tom fixed himself another cigarette. Ben took the offered packet and built himself a smoke too. The evening closed in around them as they made their way back to camp.

"Andoreana, it is time for bed."

"Just a minute more, Mama. Susie Meyers is almost done with her dinner," Andoreana said, putting the big nickel spoon against the doll's cross-stitched mouth.

Clarissa smiled at her daughter from the ancient iron stove, where she slid a bread pan into the oven. The daylight hours were too hot for baking in the summer and she often did it all after the sun went down. "All right, but soon as Susie Meyers is fed, it's up in the loft with you."

"Yes, ma'am. Did you hear what Mama said, Susie Meyers? I have to get you fed and washed up so as I can go to bed, too. Now, finish your porridge."

"Randy."

The teenager poked his head out of the little room that Franklin had built out the back of the cabin. He held an open book, and his suspenders hung down around his knees. "Yes, Ma?"

"Tonight is bread night. I'll need more wood in here."

Randy reached back to set the book atop the pine chest of drawers and came into the main room, bending his long arms through the suspenders. He hunkered down by the side of the stove to watch the red embers spark and snap through the crack in the side of the firebox. "It'll sure be nice to have a new stove, won't it?"

Clarissa dragged a sleeve across her brow. Even after sunset, baking bread was a miserable chore in the summer months. A hank of red hair tumbled across her eye. She blew at it and said, "It will be a blessing to get rid of this old fire menace."

Randy disappeared outside. Clarissa punched down a ball of dough in her mixing bowl, an edge of impatience in her voice. "Is Susie Meyers done eating yet?"

"Yes, Mama. I just have to wash her face."

"Well, make it quick, young lady. It's past your bedtime."

Andoreana pushed back her chair. She spied the bucket of water by the stove and hauled it to the table. Dipping the corner of a napkin into it, she lightly touched Susie Meyers' stitched mouth, and brushed at the doll's hands. "All done, Susie Meyers. Now it's off to bed with you." She laid the doll in a cardboard box by the wall and tucked a scrap of a wool blanket around her.

"It's off to bed with you too, Andoreana."

"All right," she replied with a note of resignation.

"And don't forget to wash *your* face and hands. I have water heating on the stove. Run a brush through your hair, too, or you'll wake up with it full of rats' nests."

Randy kicked the door open then and squeezed in sideways, his arms bowed around a bulging load of split cord wood. "Out of the way," he called, his eyes hidden behind the stack of wood.

"Watch out!" Clarissa warned, as her son drifted blindly.

"What?" Randy turned. The end of a split log swept a lamp off the top of a shelf. With a crash, the glass chimney shattered against the planks. Randy leaped aside, dropping his load, and back-peddled one step ahead of a blue flame that crawled along the floor.

Clarissa's hands leaped out of the bowl of dough. She glanced around for the bucket of water, snatched it off the table, and heaved it onto the spreading stream of fire. Immediately something told her this was wrong. The water spread the burning kerosene in a blue sheet across the wooden floor.

Randy stumbled over the logs, regained his balance, and lunged for the door to his bedroom, stepping on top of Susie Meyers and crushing her cardboard crib in the process.

Andoreana backed up against the wall, her hands pressed over her mouth, eyes bulging. She spied Susie Meyers now dangerously close to the flames. Suppressing her own fears, Andoreana sprung away from the wall, snatched up the precious doll, and darted back.

Sand, Clarissa thought, glancing around.

Sand was not a commodity she usually allowed inside her house. Something else then! At that moment, Randy reappeared. In her confusion, Clarissa couldn't be sure the boy

39

hadn't just materialized before her eyes. He flung his red-and-blue wool bed blanket over the flames and pounced upon it, beating it all over with his hands.

"Andoreana! Quick! Outside!" Clarissa bustled the little girl into the fresh night air and turned to help Randy suffocate the flames.

A small blue flame grew out of the fuzzy wool. Randy gathered the blanket up and tossed it out the door into the yard. Clarissa stomped the charred floor until every spark was dead beneath the soles of her shoes. A shovelful of dirt flew in from outside and skittered across the floor, and then another, and another, and finally Randy stepped in, wiping his forehead with a dirty hand.

"I think we got it, Ma."

Clarissa sank into a chair. Her sudden surge of energy drained in spasms as her arms clutched about her waist. A weariness pressed down on her and she heaved a sharp sigh. She stared at the dirty floor, then down at her hands, still caked in moist bread dough.

"Thank you, Lord," she breathed.

Randy put an arm over her shoulder and muttered softly, "Amen."

Andoreana peeked through the doorway. "Is it out?"

Clarissa opened her arms. Andoreana ran to her mother and was enveloped. "That was a close one, darling."

"Randy made a mess on the floor," Andoreana said.

Clarissa laughed; more a release of nervous energy than from humor. "Then we better get busy and clean it up."

Clarissa's remedy for any problem was work.

"I'll fetch the broom," Andoreana said, and as she went to the corner, she paused to pick up the crushed cardboard box. "Mama, Susie Meyers' bed is broken."

But Clarissa didn't hear. She was peering at the lump of dough in the bowl and looking at her hands, and, Andoreana thought, weeping.

Below the floorboards of the cabin, a hairline stream of kerosene spilled onto black earth and ran in a hot blue rivulet into the dried gatherings of a mouse nest, where it burned out. The nervous mouse returned to the nest where her seven pink and hairless babies squealed for her nipples.

But all was not right here.

Her sensitive nose lifted in the still, damp air. The faint odor of smoldering grass set her whiskers to twitching. Something inside her tiny brain commanded her to leave. The cries of her tiny newborns halted her steps. She looked back at the blind, helpless lumps of pink flesh, torn, as any mother would be. But the warning was insistent, overriding conflicting maternal instincts, and in the end, she scurried out from under the house and scampered into the undergrowth of the pine forest.

Four

Clarissa sat on the floor beside her daughter's bed and, in the darkness of the loft, softly sang a song she'd sung to Andoreana every night as far back as either one of them could remember.

Hush little baby, don't say a word. . . .

Andoreana was too old for such things as bedtime songs. She knew that. But it had become a ritual over the years, and rituals were important to have in a family.

Clarissa enjoyed the bit of quiet time at the end of the day with her daughter, too. After the song she listened to Andoreana's prayers, and stroked the child's fine golden hair.

"Where do you think Papa is right now?" Andoreana asked when the prayer was complete, after she had appealed to God to watch over him wherever he might be.

"Oh, Papa is probably sitting around a campfire thinking about us back here on the claim. He probably has Tad and Buttontail picketed out nearby where they have lots of green grass to munch on, and he is probably looking up at the stars right now wishing he could reach over and kiss his little Andoreana good night."

"I am not little, Mother," Andoreana said firmly.

"No, of course you're not — not anymore. You're growing up into a pretty young lady, and we are proud of you."

A pretty, young lady! It must be true. Her mama and papa had both said as much.

Andoreana sat up suddenly. "Did you remember to pack the green soap for daddy, so he can wash up before he eats?"

Clarissa smiled. "Yes, I put in a bar of soap, and a towel."

Andoreana lay her head back down, satisfied. "We got to take care of Papa," she said. She yawned and rubbed her eyes.

"Yes, we do. Good night, sweetheart," Clarissa said softly.

"Good night, Mama." Andoreana closed her heavy eyes and hugged Susie Meyers beneath the covers as her mother's footsteps receded down the ladder. She glanced once at the canvas wall of her little room glowing faintly and reassuringly from the light in the kitchen below, then shut her eyes and went to sleep thinking of her father sitting by a bright campfire with their two horses nearby.

He stirred the embers of a dying fire with

a thin stick, then snatched up the bottle of whiskey at his elbow and took a long swallow. The day had run its course like a lighted match atop a powder keg. Now at the end, it was finally beginning to look all right to him. His mood had improved some, too. The whiskey had more than a little to do with that.

"Gimme that bottle before you get it all drunk up, Neville."

Hallidae's eyes hardened past the tipped-up bottle in his hand and bore down on Turner Wilson. A trickle of whiskey traced a line over Hallidae's chin as he slowly lowered the bottle and passed it over.

Turner seized it greedily and lifted its bottom up to the lopsided crescent of a moon just visible through the treetops overhead. His throat pulsated like a reciprocating pump and, when he pulled the bottle away, a stream of whiskey spilled down the front of his duster.

Hallidae snatched the bottle back and passed it to Mcintyre. He said, "We made out okay today, but we was lucky." Hallidae glanced at each of the men. Turner sat crossed-legged across the fire from him, grinning drunkenly at the struggling flames in the growing pile of embers. At Hallidae's left, Mcintyre was sipping at the bottle just handed him. A little way off, Tom Deveraux dug earnestly through a canvas rucksack. He glanced up briefly, almost irritated with Neville's interruption, and then immediately went back to searching the bottom of the bag.

Ben Masters had his Colt revolver disassembled and spread out on an oilskin in front of him. In the light of a candle lantern he methodically ran a square of oil-soaked cloth through each hole in the cylinder.

"But we had us a mishap that I don't want to see happen again," Hallidae went on.

Ben paused in his labor over the gun and glanced up.

Hallidae's eyes held him for an instant, accusingly, and then moved back to the struggling fire. "Maybe we just got a little careless," he said easily, as if he recognized that mistakes happen to everyone and that all they needed to do was try a little harder next time.

But Ben Masters knew Hallidae better than that. Hallidae was not of the forgiving or forgetting type. He'd be watching Ben twice as close from now on. Ben thumbed the cylinder back into the pistol frame with a loud metallic click and rammed the cylinder pin in place.

"But careless or not," Hallidae was saying, "the next time someone sees any one of us in a manner what would allow them to recognize us later, that someone's gonna have to have their eyes shut — permanently." Hallidae's voice rose on that and he looked pointedly at Ben. "Do I make myself clear, Masters?"

The fat .45 cartridge in the dry rag stopped rolling between Ben's fingers. He knew Hallidae had to say it like that — had to assert his dominance now in front of these other men, but it rankled just the same. Ben inserted the cartridge into his gun and snatched up another until he had all five back in place. He snapped the loading gate shut and lowered the hammer on an empty cylinder. "You made yourself clear, Neville."

Then Tom Deveraux said, "Sheee-it!"

"What's wrong, Cotton? You lose something?" Turner said, grinning.

Deveraux glanced out of his rucksack and gave Wilson a suspicious scowl.

"You lookin' for this, maybe?" Wilson waved the tobacco pouch at him.

Across the fire from Wilson, Hallidae chuckled and stirred up the coals. Mcintyre lowered the whiskey bottle and glanced over. Ben slid his six-shooter into its holster and looked at the black man.

Tom Deveraux was up in an instant. Three long strides brought him over Wilson with shoulders bunched and his fingers bent tight into a hard fist. "That's mine," he said, his voice taut with anger. "You got no right going through my things, Wilson."

"I needed to fix me a smoke," Wilson said, grinning. "You'll get it back when I'm done with it, boy."

Deveraux's teeth came together in a flash of white. His fist darted for the pouch, but Wilson gave it a toss and it landed like a hot coal in Mcintyre's lap.

Mcintyre fumbled it up and sent it back to Wilson. "You keep me out of this, Turner."

Wilson laughed and offered the tobacco pouch up to Tom. "Here you go, boy. I reckon I'm done with fixing a smoke now."

Tom Deveraux stared at the folded chamois pouch in Wilson's hand. The big black man was shaking with anger. Slowly Ben got to his feet, ready to move out of their way if the need came.

"What's wrong, boy? Don't you want it now?" Wilson's badgering words were made brave by the whiskey. Too brave, Ben figured, sizing up the black man standing over Wilson.

"I ain't a boy," Deveraux said. He grabbed up the tobacco pouch and stomped back to his rucksack. Turner laughed and slapped his leg.

Ben let go of a long breath.

Hallidae grinned and tipped up the bottle. "You take chances."

Wilson patted the handle of the bowie at his side. "None I can't handle, Neville."

It hadn't come to blows this time, but the way Wilson rode the black man, Ben knew it was only a matter of time, and that concerned him. Tom was once again Wilson's size, but the black man didn't have Wilson's killing instincts.

"Hey, what's this?" Mcintyre said just then.

"What is what?" Ben said, slipping his holster belt over his shoulder.

"That." They followed his finger. Far out across the black sea of trees, where moonlight touched and grayed the surface, a spot of red glowed like an ember against the night.

"It looks like a fire burning way off yonder," Tom said.

Ben Masters went to his saddlebags for the brass spyglass that he had carried since spending some months as a stevedore on a Missouri River steamboat.

"Lemme see." Hallidae grabbed the spyglass away.

Ben bristled. Hallidae was carrying this show of power a bit far.

"It is a fire," Neville said after some studying. He passed the glass around for each man to take a look.

"Whatever it is that's burning, it's a long way off," Tom added.

Gauging the direction of the wind, Hallidae proclaimed that the flames posed no threat of spreading in their direction and wandered off with his bottle.

Mcintyre tapped out his mouth organ and made some noise as the night drew on. They watched the flickering point of red light on and off for more than an hour. Eventually each man made his way into his bedroll, and Ben noted just before he closed his eyes that Neville Hallidae had made a comfortable pillow out of the money sack they had taken from the bank in Buena Vista that morning.

"Andoreana . . . Andoreana!"

The voice that called her out of her dreams seemed distant, and her sleep so very deep and heavy as to be almost suffocating, as if she had rolled herself into her heavy wool blanket.

"Andoreana!"

Andoreana shrugged off the deep sleep . . . and she was coughing.

Clarissa's frantic hands had caught her up by the arms. She was dragging her from her warm bed. Andoreana didn't want to wake up. The glow on the canvas wall of her little room in the loft was brighter now than she had remembered it.

Too bright!

Andoreana could not stop coughing. Half-asleep, her hands were suddenly upon the

50

rungs of the ladder. Beneath her somewhere roared an engine of heat, like those that she imagined prowled the shining iron rails that crossed the country. Its hot breath blew up her cotton nightgown and singed her naked legs.

Her toes found the next rung down. Smoke stung her eyes. Sleep had been replaced with the sudden, horrible realization that their cabin was engulfed in flames.

"Mama!" she cried.

"Just keep moving." Clarissa's voice was near. Her words were firm, and the control in her mother's voice was somehow reassuring. Only one rung above her, Clarissa was making her way down from the loft, too. The heat billowed up her nightgown, and orange-red light flickered off her mother's legs.

Andoreana blinked at the stinging tears and coughed up the searing smoke that filled her lungs.

Then a pair of strong hands caught her up from behind and for a moment Andoreana believed that her father had returned home in time to rescue them.

He carried her out of the flames into the cool night air. When he set her on the ground, Andoreana saw that it was only Randy. He turned back to the house as Clarissa burst from the doorway and staggered out into the yard.

She fell to her knees. A violent cough wracked her body. Randy leaped to her side and helped her away from the burning cabin.

Clarissa clutched her children to herself. "We are all out?" she asked, half-dazed.

"Yes," Randy said, gulping the clean air.

Clarissa sank back to her knees. "Thank God."

Suddenly Andoreana stiffened. "Susie Meyers!"

"What?"

Andoreana broke from Clarissa's grasping fingers.

"No, darling, no!" Clarissa cried.

But Andoreana did not hear her as she darted heedlessly back into the hungry flames.

Clarissa scrambled to her feet and dove after her daughter with Randy a step behind her. The cabin was a furnace, intolerably hot with flames leaping at every turn. She caught a glimpse of Andoreana, and somehow managed to marshal the strength needed to lunge for the little girl, but she caught only a bit of nightgown.

With a crash and a gust of wind that seemed to come forth from hell, the loft collapsed in front of them, adding a shower of sparks to the hungry flames.

In the blinding heat Clarissa lost her grip on Andoreana, but somehow, through the flames, she saw the little girl stoop and rescue the doll from the glowing rubble of the loft — and then suddenly Andoreana was gone.

Clarissa cried out, her terror blinding her, and she struggled through the flames. Randy was suddenly at her side, tugging her back . . . back from the place her Andoreana had disappeared! All at once the squall of renting wood above her riveted Clarissa. She glanced up, eyes fixed and wide, and an instant later the roof came down . . .

Five

"There it is," Hallidae said, reining to a halt. Up the side of a narrow rill smoldered the gutted remains of a little cabin.

They had climbed some in elevation from their night camp. At first light, over a breakfast of coffee and boiled jerky, Neville had decided to give the town of Alpine a look. He had heard there was a bank of some note there since the railroad had hammered rails through the high pass to the new mines. Local mining companies made a practice of keeping sizable payroll accounts at such well-positioned financial establishments.

They urged their horses onto a wagon road for a closer look at the burned-out building. The heat from the blackened pile reached out to them where they drew up in the yard.

Neville swung down and walked a wide circle around the heap of charred logs. He glanced into a window where half a wall still stood. The roof had collapsed into the building at the front of the cabin. Only the door frame remained where a wedge of blue sky showed beyond its charred rectangle. The heat of the place shoved Neville back, and he came away grimacing. "Somebody didn't make it out of there."

Turner Wilson chuckled. "What a way to meet your maker. . . ." Then he thought about it a moment with his lips cocked in a crooked grin and added, ". . . or your keeper."

Ben scanned the open ground around the smoking heap. He noted Scott Mcintyre's pensive face, and Deveraux's frowning eyes and lips. His view lingered on a ragged hole that someone had dug into the hillside, then moved to a toolshed built off to one side. In a corral out back, chickens scratched at the hard ground. A pig had its snout buried in the muddied water of a galvanized tub.

Ben stepped off his horse. "I'm going to take a look around."

Neville nodded his head. "Make it quick. I don't want to spend too much time here, Ben."

Ben angled for the mine shaft. A flume built off a nearby stream ran to an old shaker box that looked broken.

Tom Deveraux swung a long leg over the saddle and dropped to the ground. "I might as well stretch some, too, while we are waitin'."

"Don't wander too far, Cotton," Neville said.

The corners of Tom's lips tightened. "I'll be nearby."

Ben stepped down into the coolness of the mine shaft. Two dozen feet back it ended at a flat wall where a pick leaned with a pair of leather gloves carefully folded over the handle. A lantern sat on an overturned nail keg, and a canteen hung from a spur of rock on the wall.

It had been a hole hard dug. Ben wanted none of the mining life for himself, yet he admired a man who would work at it as hard as the owner of this place apparently had. Ben frowned as he retraced his steps toward daylight. It was honest work. The kind of work he remembered his mother and father doing on their one hundred sixty acres that had been cut from a Missouri woodlot by sweat and brawn.

Back out in the sunlight, he turned toward the toolshed.

"Let's get moving, Ben," Neville called impatiently, stepping into his stirrup.

Ben gave the shed a grim glance. He kicked a tin can across the dusty yard and gathered up his reins. "Somebody put a lot of back into this place," he said.

"It ain't none of our concern," Neville said.

"Nope," Ben agreed.

The door to the toolshed creaked and swung half open. The four outlaws turned as a single man. A long few seconds passed. Then a little girl appeared, rubbing the morning glare from her eyes. She stood in the doorway as if afraid to step out any farther, afraid to confront the truth and the horror that stepping out of her dark hiding place would show her, Ben thought.

Turner Wilson had reached back for his revolver at the sound. Now he let his hand fall to the saddle horn and he grinned. "Well, looky here what come up out of the ashes. What they call that bird? A felix?"

"Phoenix," Tom Deveraux said.

Turner Wilson shot him a narrow glance.

Ben dropped his reins. The girl backed into the shadows at his approach. Terror was wide in her eyes. Her cheeks were smudged and her nightgown smelled of smoke. Her hands were black as Tom Deveraux's hands, and they clutched a dirty rag doll tightly.

"It's all right," Ben said gently.

Circles of soot ringed her red eyes. Tears had dried in grimy streaks down her cheeks.

"Are you hurt?"

The girl shook her head. Words seemed yet beyond her ability.

Ben put out a hand and she backed away from it as if he had extended a snake, then hesitantly she came forward. "Nobody will hurt you," Ben said. He took her into his arms and felt her body tremble.

She sobbed low against his shoulder as he carried her to where the other men waited on their horses. She choked and stared at the smoldering remains of her home as he strode past the cabin. He heard the word escape between the sobs. "Mama."

Unexpected emotion clutched at Ben's throat like a fist. He glanced at Neville, who had heard the softly spoken word too.

Wilson said, "We ain't taking the kid with us?"

"We can't just leave her," Mcintyre said, but he was unsure of himself, Ben could tell.

"The hell we can't, Fish Brain," Wilson shot back.

"Shut up, Turner," Ben snapped.

Worry was in Neville's eyes, but he voiced no objection as Ben set the girl on his saddle and swung up behind her.

"Let's put some distance between us and this," Ben said. Nothing remained here for the girl, and the decisions they needed to make now that this new wrinkle had entered their already complicated lives could best be done away from this smoking reminder of all the little girl had lost.

Their horses climbed up out of the valley of the Arkansas River, and Buena Vista became a speck upon the valley floor below.

Devon now had new warrants to add to those he already carried from Poncho Springs, Sedgwick, and Rosita. As their horses picked along the trail, he conjectured on where Neville Hallidae would turn next. Up until now Hallidae had followed an easy course that had taken him to the Arkansas River, and then north along its banks. But now it looked as if Neville had plans for some hard riding.

Devon did not look forward to a climb that could eventually take them up over the Continental Divide, yet he was not about to let these two young deputies see his weariness. He pulled himself up straight in the saddle and reined to a halt.

"Let me see that map again."

Landy reached back to his saddlebag for the dog-eared paper that was beginning to tear along its folds. "Where do you think they are heading, Marshal?"

"Your guess is as good as mine, deputy." Devon said, shaking out the paper at arm's length and craning back his head. After a moment, he said, "But if I was to make a guess, I'd count on Neville Hallidae either heading north toward Independence Pass and down into Chipita, or going straight west up over the Divide."

Devon's lips compressed to a stern line and he squinted hard against the morning sun.

There was more than enough industry up north in Chipita and Aspen to draw Neville Hallidae's attention, but the mines there were large and the banks well protected. Hallidae was already carrying cash from a string of robberies, and Devon believed that if it was another bank Hallidae was after, he'd choose one not so nearly well protected. Devon didn't think Hallidae knew he had been dogging his trail this far north, and therefore the outlaw leader would be in no great hurry to find a place to hole up in.

At least Devon hoped not.

"We will find where they made camp last night," Devon said finally. "Then I'll get a better idea what he has in mind."

Landy Peterman was a short, powerfully built man of twenty-two. He'd worked for the Chaffee County Sheriff's Department eight months now, and this was his first time on the trail of a criminal. The first time he laid eyes on Walt Devon had been four days ago when Devon stepped into his office with papers signed by Governor James B. Grant. Landy had heard by wire that Devon was coming, but he was not prepared for the tall, chiseled-faced man who had stepped through the door. Devon wore a red flannel bib shirt beneath a buttoned-up brown corduroy vest.

The marshal had the beginnings of a paunch, but he had sucked it in when he stopped in front of Landy's desk and laid papers in front of him. As he waited for the young deputy to read through them, his big, creased right hand rested casually on the bright new ivory grips of the short-barreled Colt revolver that he wore high up on his right hip.

Landy had marveled at how Devon could take the summer heat dressed as he was. Once on the trail, however, Devon made a concession to the season by unbuttoning the vest and rolling up his sleeves. The bib lay open on the left side and the shirt beneath unbuttoned. Still, the marshal seemed mostly unaffected by the heat while Landy sweated in his light cotton shirt with the sleeves cut off at the elbow. Stanley Hedstrom, in a blue collarless shirt with fine white stripes, had more than once stopped along a flowing stream to fill his canteen and soak his hair.

But Devon's concentration was forever directed at the ground, or ahead on the trail, and his ever-moving eyes seemed to miss nothing.

His five outlaws were somewhere up ahead. Landy suspected that there was no room in this man's thoughts for the heat of the day, or the hours they spent in the saddle.

Six

In a mountain meadow they drew rein and Ben helped the girl off his saddle. Wilson and Hallidae moved off to speak in low voices, and cast glances at Ben and the girl. Scott Mcintyre wandered into the trees. Tom gathered up the horses and picketed them out.

"You want something to eat?" Ben asked her. "I've got some jerked beef in my saddlebags."

Bare-footed, the girl stood clutching the doll to herself as if she did not hear him. She had said nothing as they had ridden away from the gutted cabin. Her eyes never left the smoking remains until it had dropped far out of sight. Now, almost an hour later, she had still not spoken.

"You got a name? How about I just call you 'Hey You'?"

That provoked a stare, and Ben figured it was a start in the right direction.

Scott Mcintyre stepped from the trees, buttoning his fly. "She still not talking?"

"Cat's got a mighty hold of her tongue," Ben said.

"The little girl's been through a terrible

thing," Tom said, coming back with his rucksack in hand.

"I'm not little! I am almost nine years old!"

The abruptness of her reply startled them.

"Well, she can talk after all." Tom feigned amazement. "And she'd got a drop of spunk in her, too."

Ben hunkered down. "What's your name?"

Neville and Turner came across the meadow now. Neville's expression was guarded. His eyes lingered a moment on Ben before falling upon the young girl in her soot-stained nightgown. Turner was grinning. He walked with a swagger, his arms swinging wide. He'd rolled his shirt sleeves up above his elbows and carried his hat in his left hand. "What a pretty little girl," he said.

She turned on him and stabbed him with a narrow look.

Ben tried again, "What's your name?"

Her head came around and she said, "Andoreana. Andoreana Dean."

Tom whistled. "That there is one elegant handle."

"Andoreana, Andoreana!" Turner Wilson chirped, laughing.

"I don't think I ever heard such a fancy name before," Scott commented soberly.

Ben looked back at her. "We're just simple folks here. How about we call you Andy."

Andoreana stiffened. "My name is not Andy!"

The men laughed. Neville said, "Andy is a sight less of a mouthful."

"My name is not Andy!" Defiance burned in her eyes.

"I'm kind of fetchin' with 'Andy,' myself," Wilson said. His eyes glistened and widened, and he rolled a lock of her hair in his fingers. "I ain't never before met an Andy with such pretty yellow hair."

Andoreana twisted her head free and retreated, bumping into Neville's leg.

"Hold up there, youngster," Hallidae said, catching her by the shoulders. "You ain't got no place to run off to, and I don't much care to go chasing after you."

"She don't want to be with us, Neville." Turner tried to look offended.

"Leave the kid alone; can't you see she's scared?"

"No one asked you, boy. Go tend to the horses."

Tom started at Wilson, then changed his mind. But in that uncertain moment Wilson had taken a surprised step backward — in about an equal amount that Deveraux had come forward. Wilson recovered quickly, and made a gutsy laugh when he saw that Tom did not intend to force the issue. "Anytime you want to try me, boy," he said boldly, and his hand had come to rest upon the hilt of the big bowie knife at his side.

"You two keep off each other's back," Ben said, taking Andoreana's hand before she realized what was happening. He walked her away from them and set her atop a boulder that pushed up like a gray wart through the stiff brown grass and yellow and red wildflowers. "You stay here, Andy." He grinned when he saw the anger flare in her eyes. "Better get used to it, I got a feeling it's going to stick."

"That weren't a awful smart thing to do, Ben. Taking that kid with us," Turner Wilson said when he came back.

Neville dragged the back of his hand across the coarse gray and brown stubble under his chin. "This time I have to agree with Turner," he said. "What are your intentions?"

Ben's cheeks hollowed below the sharp angle of bone. His heavy brows came together. But the question was a fair one. He was irked that he didn't have a good answer to give. "Hell, I don't know, Neville," he said low so his words didn't carry. "But we couldn't just leave her there."

"Someone would have come by eventually," Hallidae countered reasonably.

"Sure. But how long would she of had to

sit there staring at that smoking grave before they did?"

"I can't see as it was our problem. Leastwise, not till you went and made it so."

"Okay. So I made it our problem. We'll drop her off the next town we come to, and it won't cause us harm, or hardly any effort. Someone will find her kin for her, if she has any left." Ben paused then. "We'll just take care what we say in front of her."

Turner Wilson said, "You've turned us into five dandy nursemaids, Ben. I ain't so sure I care to do that." He glanced at the boulder where Andoreana sat with her knees drawn up and hugged tightly to herself.

The hem of her thin cotton nightgown moved in the slight wind, and it occurred to Ben that he'd have to come up with something more durable for the girl to wear.

But Wilson seemed to be thinking something else when he looked back at Ben. "There's only one good thing to do with a female," he said, "and it looks to me like that one over yonder is jest about old enough for what I have in mind."

The men chuckled — all but Ben.

Mcintyre said, "You'd do better to go find you an old stump-broke mare, Turner."

Tom's laugh was deep, and rumbled across the little meadow. "You just keep him away from my horses, Scott."

Suddenly they were all laughing.

"I saw a broken-down plug back at Buena Vista on our way out," Neville Hallidae added.

Even Turner Wilson had begun to grin.

Ben Masters felt the tension ease.

"I don't do old plugs, Neville," Turner said, "but I'd surely be interested in taking some lessons if'n you'd care to teach . . . or maybe Fish Brain here would want to demonstrate to us just how it's done down Texas way."

Scott Mcintyre stopped laughing. "Aw, we was only funnin' you, Turner."

Neville stopped laughing too. "We still haven't decided what to do with her."

"Like I said, we'll drop her off the next town."

"And in the meantime?"

Ben gathered his thoughts a minute before his bushy brown mustache made a hitch above his grin. "I guess in the meantime we keep her away from Turner."

When the laughter died down, Neville said, "All right, but she's your responsibility. And she better not figure out what we are about." This last advice was spoken with no humor, and its tone quickly sobered them all.

They made camp that night in a high valley. A stream rushed down from the naked peaks just above them. Scattered about were the ruddy red and yellow piles of rubble scratched up out of the earth by the prospector's pick. The land was being ravaged, Ben thought. If the gold seekers had already made it this far into the wilderness, he wondered what another fifty years would bring.

"It will all be as flat as Missouri someday," he said aloud to himself as his eye traced the ragged line of pockmarks strung out along the stream and up the valley.

"What will be flat like Missouri?" Tom asked.

Ben hadn't realized that Deveraux had come up behind him. He said, "All this. The way folks are coming out here to dig up the mountainside, I reckon it won't be but fifty years before they manage to level all of it."

Tom laughed. "They'll never level this country. Not in fifty years, not in fifty thousand years. Now what you need is a river — and I mean a *river* like the Mississip' — if you want to do some levelin'. They call it erosion, and it takes the most awful long time. Maybe five million years?" Tom eyed Ben. "Why you lookin' at me like that?"

"Five million years? Where'd you hear that?"

"I didn't hear it nowhere. I read it in a book by a writer feller named Ingersoll."

Ben extended his brass spyglass and studied

the piles of tailing, one after the other, until they disappeared beyond the curve of the valley. His view came back and lingered a moment on a ground squirrel sitting atop a chunk of yellow rock thrown up by a gold hunter's pick.

"Five million years, you say?" The squirrel flicked its tail and leaped into the shadows. Ben looked back at Tom Deveraux's wide white eyes and flashing teeth.

"If it's a day."

"Humm. Well, then I won't worry about it just yet."

Tom laughed and continued on down to the stream with the canteens swinging enthusiastically at his side. Ben looked for Andy and found her watching Neville and Scott hauling deadfalls to feed their fire later on. He remembered what he had come for, replaced the spyglass, and dug the oilcloth package out of his saddlebags.

"Come on over here, Andy," he said, finding a downed tree to sit on.

She had been crying, he could see, and she struggled mightily now not to show her tears.

Ben patted the tree next to him and she climbed up.

"You want to tell me what happened back there?" he asked as he unwrapped the

69

package on his legs.

Her shoulders rolled beneath the flimsy nightgown. She looked at her dirty hands that clutched the rag doll on her lap, careful that he should not see her eyes. "I don't know for sure, Mr. Masters. I think it was the lamp."

"You got to be careful with lamps," Ben said. He peeled back the oilcloth and shooed away a fly that lit on the lump of hard jerky. Then he fished around inside his pocket.

"My brother, Randy . . ." Her voice faltered. She struggled again to keep her emotions from bursting out once more, showing more control than Ben figured a child rightly ought to. "My brother, Randy, he knocked over the lamp while carrying in the wood. It was bread night, you see."

She paused and studied him to make sure he did see.

"Hu-huh." Ben opened his pocket knife and frowned at the blade in the afternoon light. "And that's what started the fire?"

"No."

He looked at her.

"I mean, well . . . not right away, you see. Mama and Randy had the fire out, but I guess maybe it took to smoldering under the cabin. It weren't the stove like Papa worried so. Mama made sure it was out cold every night before she went to bed. So, it must have been the lamp. . . ."

Her words trailed off. Ben heard the low whimper. He wanted to wrap an arm around the child, but something inside him made that impossible. He thought of his own sister again and wondered if she had someone to give her comfort when she needed it. He saw Rita's face whenever he looked at Andy. Rita would be almost twenty now, but the face he remembered that day he left the farm belonged to a nine-year-old girl, and Andy conveniently fit the part.

She sniffed, dragged a filthy finger under her eye, and said, "When Mama shook me awake, the smoke was already so heavy that it choked me and burned my eyes. I remember the bright flames, and Mama pushing me down the loft ladder. The heat was like a furnace at my back . . . and then Randy carried me outside and we coughed up the smoke and . . ." She stopped and looked out across the valley.

"Then you all made it out of the cabin?" Ben asked.

Andy found something to stare at and did not hear him. At least that was the impression Ben got. But after a moment he saw her head shake slowly, sadly.

"No," she said in a choked whisper. She

buried her face into the dirty rag doll that she clutched as if it was gold and diamonds.

Ben's lips twitched into a frown. He turned to the jerky and worked the knife through it, carving a thick slice from the hard lump, and then another . . . and then he didn't hear Andy's whimpering, and when he looked, she was staring at the knife.

"Here is something to eat," Ben said, offering her a piece of the hard meat.

"Did you wash that knife?"

"What?"

"Don't you wash your knife before cutting your food?"

Ben looked at the blade, and then at her, and shook his head. "No . . . no, I guess I don't."

"Then I don't want any, thank you," she said, and made a muddy streak under her eye with her finger.

Seven

Andoreana huddled against the cool of the evening. The wind had needle-sharp teeth that bit through her cotton nightgown and dragged from her a long, violent shiver. She tried hugging Susie Meyers tighter, but there was no warmth to be found in the doll, not like the warmth she had once known in her mother's arms, or Randy's smile.

The tears came again. A flood of them that she could not hold back. Something within told her that she had made a poor trade in that thoughtless plunge back into the flames to rescue Susie Meyers. But her child's brain refused to grasp and hold on to the full import of that thought . . . in the end, all she had to cling to was the doll, and she did so with an ardor that defied the strength in her young body.

A sharp crack brought her head about.

By the fire, Neville Hallidae snapped a dried branch beneath his boot and fed it into the flames under the fire-blackened pot where dinner boiled.

Andoreana was hungry. Yet she had only just begun to feel empty pangs in her stomach through the numbing pain that had throttled her heart all day. But now the odor of cooking food was unbearable. Even more than the food, though, she longed for her father's arms about her — strong, comforting, absolutely dependable.

She saw Ben Masters a short distance away, cross-legged upon the ground working over his saddle with thread and awl. Mr. Masters tried to be nice to her, and she liked him. But his concern for her could not take the place of her father's arms. She liked the Negro, Tom, too. She did not like Turner Wilson, nor did she care for the look of displeasure she saw in Neville Hallidae's eyes whenever he thought that she was not watching.

Scott Mcintyre was another story. He treated her well enough, but there was something about him, some weakness within him, that she could not put a finger on, something beneath his broad shoulders and his obvious physical strength.

Andoreana turned back toward the fire, drawn by movement there. Neville Hallidae crossed to the tree that Tom Deveraux had chosen to lounge against and toed the black man in the side none too gentle.

Tom's head came up out of the book open upon his knees. Impatience etched itself on his broad black face, and more than just a little irritation with it. Andoreana watched the lines of strain work themselves out of the big man's face as he got a grip on that irritation.

"Well, ain't that the life? A man of leisure, here, reading his book in the cool of the evening."

Tom straightened up. "The last thing I figured we all needed was another cook bent over that pot, Neville."

"That's what *you* figured?" Hallidae nodded his head at the book. "What you reading there?"

Tom held it up so that Neville could see the spine. Andoreana watched his lips move. After some struggle he said, "*The Adventures of Huckleberry Finn?* What's it about?"

"A runaway colored and a white boy. You ought to read it."

Neville grunted. "I don't read nigger trash, Cotton. You put that thing away now and get us some more wood." He wheeled away toward the stream, pausing only long enough to give Ben Masters a quick look.

Ben didn't see it, but Andoreana did. She wondered what the problem was between these two. She had a good idea that her being here was part of it.

What were these men doing up here anyway? She was pretty sure they weren't prospectors. Andoreana knew the look of miners and these five had none of the signs about them. And they weren't at all like the buck-aroos she had seen on the trip west, with their wide hats and flapping . . . *chapareros?* She half remembered her father explaining the word to her.

But they did wear guns, and they seemed most comfortable with them. She didn't know many miners — or many men at all, for that matter — who wore a gun all the time. Except maybe lawmen. Somehow, these five did not strike her as lawmen.

In those precious moments when her mind was able to leave behind the horrible truth of her mother and brother's death, Andoreana watched these men, and listened to their talk, and she wondered.

Tom closed the book on his lap after care-fully marking his place with a blade of dry grass and tucked it into his rucksack. He stood, stiff from a day in the saddle, glanced narrowly at Neville Hallidae's receding form, then ambled away toward the thick stand of trees that followed a rill down to the stream.

Andoreana caught Turner Wilson's eyes on her, and all at once had a feeling like she'd walked into a spider's web. Turner's lips crept up into a thin smile. She shivered and looked away, not sure why he disturbed her so, but suddenly very sure that she didn't want to be alone with him. More than anything, she wished her father would ride up the valley at this very moment and take her up in his arms, and carry her away with him.

He kicked at the dead ashes of the campfire and tilted his head back, squinting against the splintered rays of a sun dying against the darkening trees. The land climbed to the west, and even in the lengthening shadows beneath the tall ponderosa pines, it was clear that Neville Hallidae's tracks headed off in that direction. Devon heard Landy come up behind them.

"I found another cigarette butt, Marshal."

Devon glanced at the stub of paper in Landy's fingers. "Well, that's one more for your collection," was all he said. He strode away onto a path that angled away to the east, lowering to one knee to study a heel print there. Wide and rounded . . . one of the bootprints he'd been cataloging, all right. The foot path ended abruptly at a rock outcropping where the land fell away and the Arkansas Valley spread out below. Buena Vista was a smear upon the valley floor, and beyond, the land rose steeply up out of the valley in a vertical upthrust.

They had ridden along that very ridge of high ground yesterday, following Hallidae's faint trace that at times disappeared upon the hard, rocky soil. But here, on this side of the valley, the trees were thicker and the ground softer. Tracking would not be nearly as difficult.

Just the same, it had been a hard ride. Walter Devon thought fondly of the growing web of steel rails radiating out from civilization, reaching back even as far as this valley. Unfortunately, Neville Hallidae wasn't following the railway lines, and horseback was the only way to follow him.

Devon arched his back. His spine popped in half a dozen places. He spied a piece of paper caught in the branches of a piñon pine a little distance below the outcropping and eased himself down to gather it up. A grin cracked the leather of his face.

"Here's another one," he said to Landy when he returned to the old campsite.

Landy took it eagerly, and carefully added it to the paper where nearly a dozen cigarette stubs were already collected.

"Tell me, deputy, what are you planning on doing with all those things?"

"Evidence," he said, surprised that the question needed asking.

Devon gave a short laugh. "That's what they must call modern police work." He stepped back up into the stirrup.

Stanley Hedstrom looked pained. "You mean we aren't stopping here for the night?"

Devon turned and Stanley knew from the look in the old marshal's eyes the answer he'd get. Hedstrom frowned resignedly, gathered up the reins, and climbed wearily back onto the horse's back.

"I was just thinking about the horses," he said lamely. "They've been doing a lot of climbing today, you know."

"I know, deputy." There was a grin on Devon's face as he turned back and nudged his horse forward. "We still have a good hour of daylight left in this day," he said, picking up the trail, "and Neville Hallidae isn't going to make it any easier on us tomorrow."

"Slave driver," Hedstrom whispered to Landy as he fell in behind.

The grin on Devon's face widened ever so slightly.

Eight

"Come get it while it's hot," Wilson said, banging the bottom of a burned pan. The coagulated brown goo that he ladled out of the black pot clung to a twisted nickel silver spoon and dripped thickly into battered blue-enameled cups. The men wandered in, none too anxious. Andoreana came up alongside Ben.

"Here, you get in front," Ben said, making room for her.

The tin cup Turner thrust into her hand was hot, and she dashed for a spot of ground to set it down upon, blew across her fingers, and rubbed her palms together. Then she sat there looking around with some dismay while the men made tentative advances at the thick substance in their cups.

"What's wrong, Andy?" Ben said, settling cross-legged down beside her. "I know it's not home cooking, but it'll fill you, and it won't harm you." He gave her a friendly wink. "At least, it hasn't hurt any of us so far."

She looked around at the men spooning down their dinner and she said, "Aren't we going to say grace before we eat?"

The rattling of spoons ceased so swiftly that one might have thought she'd announced that she was a duly sworn-in constable of the law. They looked at each other as if waiting for the final line in a hilarious joke.

"At home we always thank the Lord for the blessings of good food."

This was no joke. This was serious! The kid meant it! A low snicker moved through their ranks. Ben grinned too, but put on a sober face when her eyes turned on him in all seriousness.

"Don't you say grace before you eat?"

"Not as a general rule," Hallidae said. For some reason which Andoreana did not understand, this caused considerable laughter among the men.

"Can't say as I ever said grace," Wilson said.

Tom Deveraux considered the question. "I remember my mam giving thanks before a meal. Though what she had to be thankful for, I still haven't figured out. We ate mostly the leavings, but sometimes we'd get an old cow what died out in the field." Tom laughed. "It is truly surprising how many of them cows just up and died for no reason at all."

"I'm surprised they didn't run out of cows," Scott said.

Tom winked. "We ain't so thick-headed like some folks would like to think."

"My folks said a blessing before a meal," Ben said.

Andoreana took her cue from him. "I'll say it, if you want me to."

There was a burst of laughing.

"Let the kid say it," Neville said, cutting short their merriment. "We wouldn't want Andy to get the wrong idea about us, would we, boys?"

The mirth subsided into trickles of restrained humor. Andy lowered her head and folded her hands. The men seemed to suffer from a sudden stiffness in their necks but, with some effort, managed to get their eyes down a notch.

"Dear Jesus, thank you for this food. Bless it to the nourishment of our bodies. Thank you also for these nice men who have helped me, and please watch over each and every one of them. And please let Papa find me soon. Amen."

When she finished, Hallidae's eyes were fixed upon her in a wary scowl. "Your father is still alive?"

"Yes," she said. "He was away at Colorado Springs, to buy us a new cook stove — one with a three-gallon hot water tank. He'll come looking for me as soon as he comes back."

Hallidae shifted the scowl to Ben Masters, but he spoke to Andoreana. "Then we can

82

expect him to be following us."

"Oh, yes."

"Sheee-it," Tom said fervently.

Andoreana looked at him, startled.

Tom set his food aside and walked down to the stream.

"What's wrong with him?" Wilson asked.

Ben shrugged his shoulders.

Andoreana looked at her hands and made a face. "I can't eat with these. May I please have some soap?"

"Soap?" Ben pulled his eyes off Tom's hulking shape tramping down to the water and looked at her.

"We don't have any," Hallidae said flatly.

"How do you wash your hands? How do you wash your dishes?"

"We don't, kid."

Andoreana had trouble understanding this. Her eyes turned down at the spoon sticking out of the beans and discovered crusted food gathered there in the ornate scrolling engraved into the handle. All at once, she was no longer hungry.

"I do believe I have some soap someplace," Mcintyre said, standing. He rummaged through his saddlebags and came back with a leather pouch tied up with a thong. "Here we go." He worked the knot loose and unrolled the pouch. "You can have it to wash your hands with."

"Thank you, Mr. Mcintyre," she said, peeking in at the green lump that had long ago fused to the side of the pouch. She worked it loose and stared at it, uncertain. But it *was* soap. Strong, green, and it smelled clean despite its appearance. "I'll go wash my hands right now."

She tried working it into a lather in the cold water, but the green lump was not very good soap, she decided. Not like the lye soap her mother had made. Tom Deveraux was suddenly standing at her side.

"Hello, Mr. Deveraux."

He didn't answer at first. Struggling with a bit of hesitation, he came closer by a single step and stopped as if an impenetrable wall separated them.

"Andy?" he said in his deep voice that at once could be booming, and the next moment low and resonant. She liked its sound. It had strength, like her father's.

"Mr. Deveraux?"

Tom went down on his haunches and fumbled a smooth river rock in his oversized fingers. She remembered a day a year or so back when her father had come home late after her mother had waited up most the night for him. Her father had had just that same tone in his

84

voice when he spoke, and his fingers had worried the brim of his hat. She hadn't known what the trouble was then, only that it was something bothersome to adults, not to kids. Of course, that was back when she was still a kid. Now she felt she ought to know the reason for his trepidation.

"I've treated you good, haven't I?"

"Sir?"

"I mean, I haven't . . . touched you."

"No, Mr. Deveraux."

"I haven't hurt you, have I?"

"No. No one here has hurt me."

Her answers seemed to please him. His lips worked up a small smile. "Good, good. You just remember to tell the truth if anyone should ask you — you know, like your pap, or maybe a marshal, if he should ask."

"I always tell the truth, Mr. Deveraux. It is a sin to tell a lie."

Tom grinned at her. "That's true, chil', but maybe sometimes it's okay to tell just a little lie, ain't it?"

Andoreana shook her head. "No. My papa says lying is always wrong."

"You mean to say you never tell a lie?"

"No, sir. At least none that I know of."

Tom shook his head. "You certainly are a proper little girl, Andy."

"Yes, sir. Only, I'm not little anymore. And

my name is Andoreana."

Kathleen Hamil toyed with the empty teacup before setting it down carefully on the white crocheted tablecloth. "It still gives me the shakes to think about it," she said finally, peering into the wide concerned eyes across the table from her. In the other room she could hear Peter rummaging around, and then he was standing in the doorway. Tall, strong, handsome — so much like her own George had been. She had always thought both men shared many of the same good traits — and why not? She and her sister, Marie, were so close they would naturally choose men of similar qualities. Peter stood in the light of a coal oil lamp, methodically packing his pipe just as George did.

"You don't have to talk about it now if you don't want to, Kath," Peter said around the stem of the pipe. He struck a match against the iron match holder and put it to the bowl, drawing in deeply.

Marie added, "That's right. You can have all the time you need. And whenever you feel like talking, we will be ready to listen."

"You both are so understanding about this. I don't know how I'd handle it without you."

Marie touched Kathleen's hand, then went to the stove to tend to the impatient teapot.

"Another cup, Kath?"

Kathleen pushed her cup across the table-cloth. "It happened so suddenly, I can scarce put all the pieces together. One minute I was talking to Mr. Deeder, and the next, four masked men were waving revolvers at us and demanding our money."

Marie shook her head and clucked disapprovingly. "It's the sort of thing you read about. You never expect it to happen to you."

Kathleen hugged back a cold shudder. "And then that horrible man taking all the money I had left in the world. Money my George worked hard for, and the little that his father left him when he had died. Everything we had. Gone.

"After the sheriff got us out of the safe and questioned us, a marshal and his deputies showed up and asked us the same questions all over again. It turns out we were robbed by a desperado named Neville Hallidae. The marshal said he'd been following them from the New Mexico Territory, and he expected they'd cause more mischief before he caught up with them."

Marie brought the tea to the table and spooned in sugar for both of them.

"Well, of course, that's why I missed the train."

Peter sat across from her. "Your telegram

certainly upset us, Kath. We're just thankful that you aren't hurt. Lisa was up most the night with nightmares. But you know how kids are, the next day she was climbing the tree and looking for the smoke of your train."

Kathleen held back the surge of emotion; no, she did not know how kids were, and with George gone . . .

She submerged her despair and fixed a tilted smile upon her face, but Peter had sensed her sudden plunge.

He cleared his throat. "I'd best be getting back to the forge and see how Clearance is making out." He grabbed up his hat and, as he started for the door, said, "See you two at dinner." Then he was gone. Kathleen caught a glimpse of him through the window, striking out across the street to the blacksmith shop with his name across the wide double doors.

Silence filled the kitchen, as if each woman was listening to Peter's receding footsteps echo in her mind. Then Marie said, "Kath. You know you have a home with us as long as you want it."

Kathleen smiled thinly. "I know that."

"And as for money, Peter and I don't have much, what with him just opening up his new business, but I know that Mr. McKormick is looking for someone to work the counter. You'd be perfect for the job with your way with yard goods. If you like, I'll take you over right now."

Kathleen Hamil thought it over, and then with sudden determination, she stood and set her teacup down with a thump. "It's what Mother did, isn't it, Marie? And she with three children. Let's go see this Mr. McKormick."

"I'll get my hat."

Marie hurried into the next room and returned, working a purple ribbon into a bow beneath her chin.

"You know, Marie," Kathleen said, "the worst thing is not the loss of the money, or even the fright of seeing all those revolvers pointed at you. The worst thing is that when someone forces himself on you it's almost like . . ."

Her words caught. She drew in a deep breath and with resolve said, "It's almost like being violated."

Marie's eyes expanded. "That's awful, Kath. You poor dear." And she put an arm around her sister.

Kathleen pulled away. Her face was set with resolution, and ice glistened in her brown eyes. "One thing for sure, Marie, I'll never forget that face — those dark eyes, those sharp cheekbones, that mustache. That horrible face! I shall carry a vision of it to my grave, I shall!"

Kathleen put her own hat on, settling it in place with a firm twist. The black ribbon flew into a bow, and she and Marie stepped out into the streets of Pitkin to pay Kelvin McKormick a visit.

Nine

Night came on with a suddenness, as it does in the mountains, and only the valiant efforts of a blazing fire prevented its shadowy shroud from drawing over them completely. Ben paused at the rim of firelight, and as he stood there looking down at his saddle, he could hear the stream off to his left. The clear and cold sky showed only a thin slice of moon, and the Milky Way arched like a wide band of ice crystals. Their camp, this mountain, the whole world, seemed to stop at this very point where the firelight reached its limit. It was useless to venture out on a dark night like this, and besides, the chill breeze off the tall peaks above them tended to keep a man near his fire.

Ben came back with his blanket roll and an extra woolen shirt. Andy was huddled by the fire, but even its friendly flames could not keep the cold from stabbing through her thin nightgown.

"First thing, we got to get you some decent clothes, Andy," Ben said. "I know about two of you can fit in this shirt, but we won't judge a style contest tonight." He smiled at her, and got a halfhearted grin in return.

Andy shoved her arms up the sleeves. Ben could hear her teeth rattling, and when she had the shirt buttoned up, the tail hung down below her knees.

"Thank you," she chattered.

"And if you intend to get any sleep tonight, you'll need this blanket too."

"But what about you?" she protested.

"I've got a wool coat. I'll make out, all right?"

"What you got for me, Ben?" Turner Wilson piped in.

Desultory laughs made their way round the fire. Tom threw in another chunk of wood.

Turner went on, "Andy can sleep with me. I'll surely do my best to keep the little gal warm."

"I'm not little."

Turner laughed. "That will make it all the more interesting."

"Lay off the kidding," Scott said. "You'll scare her."

"I don't scare nobody. I'm just a warm, cuddly fellow, ain't that right, Andy?"

She glanced at Ben for an explanation of the words and the meanings that passed above her head; meanings that seemed plain to the men about her.

"Don't pay him no mind. Turner runs off

at the mouth sometimes. Like a mongrel dog that got himself a bellyful of bad food."

Sudden anger narrowed Turner's eyes. "You prepared to prove up them words, Spyglass?"

"I don't know as I have to prove 'em up, Turner," Ben said easily. "Everyone here knows they're true." Ben settled to the ground next to Andy and helped her work the blanket over her shoulders.

"Sit down and shut up," Neville Hallidae said.

Turner Wilson shot a glance at Hallidae. Firelight played across the outlaw leader's face in a patchwork of shifting shadows. It was an unsmiling face, reflecting troubled thoughts.

Andy said to Ben, "My papa would say he was gargling his throat with axle grease."

Tom choked back a laugh.

"Cute, kid," Turner said. "See if I treat you nice anymore." He retreated into the darkness and returned with a bottle of whiskey.

Ben opened his pocket knife. "See, I spent some time sharpening it, Andy." He held the blade in the dancing firelight. "Then I took it down to the stream and gave it a good washing." Ben brought out his cache of jerky and slivered off a piece. "I'll bet you're about half starved by now."

"Yes, I am," she said. She took the meat as if it had come from the last cow on earth. Ben felt an unusual swell of satisfaction in his chest.

"I done gave her beans. If she's hungry, it's her own damn fault," Turner said.

"But your dishes were all dirty, Mr. Wilson."

"Little Miss Fuss and Feathers. You best get used to them being that way if you expect to eat around here." Wilson lifted the bottle to his lips.

"My papa says a corkscrew never pulled a man out of a hole."

Wilson choked and shot her a glance. "I'm getting real tired hearing what your papa says." And he took his bottle away to the privacy of his bedroll in the shadows.

"Try not to rile him too much, Andy," Ben advised.

"But I wasn't trying to."

Ben grinned. "For not trying, you're sure doing a fine job of it."

The spade bit into the tenacious earth with a hard, cold rattle, a funeral dirge that fell upon numbed ears. With each bite the hole grew deeper and wider. And for every shovelful, a tear moistened the rocky ground.

Franklin Dean scraped out two shallow

graves and walked a dazed track back to the remains of his home, fighting down a sudden surge of bile as he carefully lifted the charred remains of his wife up onto the blanket and folded it over. Despite the cruel butchery of the flames, Clarissa had been his wife, and he cherished the rolled-up blanket that now weighed half of what it might have two days earlier.

He came back for Randy, and struggled with different and deeper emotions. Clarissa had been his wife, but Randy his flesh and blood. The wicked edge of pain was enough to lift his heart from his chest, still warm and beating.

Franklin Dean did what had to be done. His brain retreated to an empty haven where it no longer registered his grief. To do so now, Franklin was certain he would die from the pain. Just the same, there was a voice ringing out like a church bell inside his head — there were only two bodies here! And search as he might, he had found no trace of Andoreana. That hope alone sent a surge of vitality to his muscles as he shoveled the hard-won rocky soil back into the holes.

He cursed himself for allowing that stove to remain in the house. And he cursed himself again; if only he'd taken his family along with him as Andoreana had asked. If only he had forbidden Clarissa from using the stove. If only . . .

Franklin bore the full indictment upon himself with each shovelful that fell with a dull thud upon the blankets. He finished the grim task and was staring at the mounds that represented two thirds of his life when he became aware of the sound of horses coming up behind him.

His back stiffened. He remembered the Winchester beneath the seat of the wagon, and faulted himself again for having left it behind, forgotten the moment he'd reined to a stop in the yard. Fingers clenching the shovel in his hand, Franklin wheeled about, squinting into the low morning sunlight beyond the riders that stood watching.

"Whoooa, there, friend," the man astride a tall horse said, holding up a hand. "We intend you no harm." On either side of him rode two younger men, but it was plain this big fellow with graying hair and unshaven face was in charge.

"Who are you?" Franklin Dean demanded.

Devon thumbed back the lapel of his vest, showing the scuffed and tarnished glint of a badge. "My name is Walter Devon, Deputy Federal Marshal, *temporarily* attached to the state of Colorado. This here is Landy Peterman and Stanley Hedstrom. They're with the

Chaffee County Sheriff's Department. I'm on the trail of a band of yahoos up from the Territories, led by a man named Hallidae. They crossed the state line a couple weeks ago and helped themselves to some honest folk's money. I intend to bring 'em before Judge Frank Springer's court in the New Mexico Territory."

Landy gave Devon a sideways glance. "They're in Colorado now, Marshal. We catch them here, they go before a Chaffee County judge."

Walt Devon gave him a thin smile and said to Franklin Dean, "I see you've had a hard time here." He nodded at the two new graves. "Is there anything we can do to help?"

Dean shook his head and lowered the shovel. "It's all been done. All except for the markers. I'd like to say a few words, but the Bible went with the house."

Devon reached into his saddlebags and came back gripping a small dog-eared Bible. "You can use this one."

Landy gave a surprised look — he'd have been less startled to see the old marshal draw a live and fighting bobcat from his saddle pouch than that book.

"Thank you, Marshal," he said and thumbed through it to a passage that he seemed to have in mind.

Devon nodded at his deputies to dismount, and removed his hat and halted a few paces behind the bowed man.

After the short service, Franklin brought them to a spring that formed a rivulet down to the larger stream where he worked his placer claim. Devon and his deputies drank of the cool water and soaked their hats.

Devon told Franklin that Hallidae's trail passed right by his place.

"Hallidae?" Franklin stared at the burned remains of his home. "I thought it was the stove," he said to himself, and then suddenly, "Andoreana!" A half-crazed look came to his eyes. "My daughter, Andoreana. She wasn't —" The words stuck in his throat. He pointed at the burned cabin. "I mean, her body wasn't there. This . . . this Hallidae Gang must have happened upon my place, burned it, and then taken Andoreana!"

Devon settled the damp hat back on his head, and his hand came to rest on the ivory pistol grips at his hip as he thought this over. "That doesn't seem to be their way of doing things, Mr. Dean. Neville Hallidae has never taken a hostage far as I know, and with the three banks in Colorado that they robbed, no one was hurt."

"But it must be true!" Franklin's eyes

flamed with urgency. "They must have taken Andoreana; otherwise, she'd be here, waiting for me. Don't you see! Andoreana is a bright girl. She wouldn't wander off by herself. She knew I'd return for her. No! This Hallidae Gang has taken her. Heaven knows what they intend to do with her!"

"Ease back, Dean. I know these fellows. I don't aim to defend what they have done, but before I'd accuse them of what I think you are accusing them of doing, I'd want to hear it from your little girl's own lips."

"How can you say that? They're criminals! You said so yourself. You're hunting them for robbing banks!"

"That's right — robbing banks. Not molesting little girls."

"You can stand there and defend them, Marshal, but I'm getting my rifle and going after them!" Franklin pushed past into the yard and unhitched the team from his wagon.

Devon drew in a heavy breath and held it a moment before coming to a decision. "Go give him a hand with his horses, Landy."

"But, Marshal, we aren't going to let him come with us?"

"He'll either ride with us, or we'll be crosswise with him the whole way. Which would you rather it be — him working with us, or against?"

Landy nodded his head unhappily. "In other words, it's better to have him where we can keep an eye on him."

"I'd say that was the lesser of two evils."

Landy had to agree.

"Hedstrom. Bring the horses over," Devon said, turning to his other deputy. "Give them water before we head out."

They gathered together in the yard. Franklin tossed a saddle over one of his horses and turned the other loose in the corral after forking in enough hay to keep the animal until he returned. He took his Winchester from under the wagon seat and swung up into the saddle.

Landy and Hedstrom mounted up while Devon retrieved his Bible and tucked it back into his saddlebag.

"I didn't know you read the Bible, Marshal," Hedstrom said.

Devon stepped into the stirrup and lifted himself onto his saddle, muffling a low grunt. "I don't, deputy. Leastwise, not often," he said, settling into the worn seat.

"Then why do you carry it?"

Devon grinned and the lines deepened at the corners of his eyes. "It reminds me of my place in all of this, deputy," he said. "You see, out in the territory, I'm the only law there is, and I have only one person to answer to for what I do." Devon hitched a thumb over his shoulder at the saddlebag. "I carry that book there to remind me just who that one person is."

Devon turned his animal away from the burned-out cabin, and the growing company of riders fell in behind.

Ten

Ben awoke the next morning cold and stiff. When he glanced over at where Andy had fallen asleep the night before, he saw that she was gone. He stood, working the kinks from his back and looked around. A cool mist hung in the air, softening the harsh landscape and thickening in the valley where prospectors' picks had turned the land over like some Goliath-sized gopher gone mad.

But Andy was not around.

Ben hunched down by the dead fire. There was still warmth beneath the white ash there. He spread his hands over it, allowing the latent heat to work into his fingers and knuckles, then he snapped twigs to feed to the embers that grew out of the ashes where his breath fanned them.

Hallidae groaned and threw aside his blanket, sitting up stiffly. He rolled his head back on his neck and said, "Getting too old for this, Ben." He walked with the stiff-legged gait of a man who had spent too many nights dodging rocks and pine cones. "Got a fire going?"

"Working on it. Andy is gone."

"Gone?" Hallidae looked over at her rumpled blanket. "Likely out seeing to nature. No place for her to go to up here. She'll turn up once she smells breakfast."

Ben grinned. "I wouldn't count on that. She's a persnickety tyke. Like as not she got it in her head to hoof it back down to her home — what's left of it."

"You're taken with the kid, aren't you, Ben?"

"Somebody has got to look out for her."

"Sure, but it's more than that with you."

Ben pulled thoughtfully at the solid beginnings of a beard. "She reminds me of my kid sister, Neville. Rita was about Andy's age when I left home. I haven't seen or even thought much of her in over ten years."

Neville's expression clouded, and Ben could not read the dark eyes that studied him. "You're not thinking of pulling out on me, are you? 'Cause if you are, it could make things mighty hot between us. We've had some words of recent. I'd not like to see it go beyond that."

It occurred to Ben that pulling out was exactly what he'd been thinking, only he had not recognized the thoughts. Neville's words brought Ben's feelings into clear focus. He recovered in an instant and put an easy smile on his face. "Hell, Neville, don't we all think of leaving from time to time?"

The uncertainty in Neville's face eased. "Yeah, guess we all do . . . from time to time. I'll get us some water for coffee while you work on that fire." Neville reached back for the coffeepot and discovered it gone. He looked around. "What did you do with the pot?"

"It should be over there with Wilson's Dutch oven and skillet." Even as Ben spoke, he saw that the skillet and oven and coffeepot were not where he'd seen them the night before. "Well, they were right there. . . ."

They looked at each other and Ben said, "Andy!" And even as he spoke, Ben heard a distant clink and clatter coming from the direction of the stream.

Andy was scrubbing away at Turner Wilson's black Dutch oven with a handful of sand when Ben and Neville came up. Their footsteps brought her head around, and a smile, almost as bright as the morning sunshine climbing up over the nearer peaks, greeted them. But Ben saw the red circles around her eyes. Andy had been crying.

Ben grinned. "I see you took it on yourself to get things washed proper around here. You always up with the sun?"

"I couldn't sleep," she said lamely. "I had a bad dream." She sighed. "Whenever Mama couldn't sleep, she would get up and go to work. 'Work keeps a restless brain happy,' she used to say."

"You're liable to come upon a bear if you wander away from camp," Neville said sternly, though there was a hint of a smile on his lips.

"I looked all around before I left. And besides, I was making so much noise that no bear would ever come upon me by accident. Papa says the only time a bear will hurt you is if you startle him, or threaten a she-bear with cubs."

"Your papa says that?"

"Yes, sir, Mr. Hallidae."

"Humm."

Ben said, "Your papa is pretty smart when it comes to animals."

"Oh, he is. He tracks bear and deer, and is always off hunting in the winter when the stream is frozen over, or it's too cold to work. Mama would say, 'Franklin, you could find a snowy owl on a winter morning.' And he'd say, 'Oh Clarissa, stop filling the children's heads.' "

Andy blinked. The smile disappeared. She looked back at the iron pot in her hand, then quickly turned her head away. "And he will come and find me, too," she said softly.

Hallidae glanced at Ben, a black scowl of concern on his face. Ben knew the sooner they dropped Andy off where she could be cared for, the better it would be for her.

Turner Wilson came up behind them, hitching a dirty gray suspender up over his left shoulder. "What we got here? You three conspiring to rob a bank or something?" he said, grinning.

The quick glance that Neville gave Turner cut off his glib patter, but the grin remained. His view lowered to Andy, and in a glance he saw all their pots and pans and knives and forks. Some were laid out bright and shiny on the rocks near the water, others submerged in a little pool formed by three round stones arranged along the edge.

His grin curled instantly into rage. "What the hell are you doing!" The suddenness of it caught Andy off guard, and even Neville looked surprised. Ben wheeled at the explosion in time to see Wilson's crazed eyes widen.

"You're ruining them! You're scraping all the seasoning out of that iron!"

"I am not," Andy came back. "I'm only scraping out the leavings of all your old meals." She tried to keep a respectful tone, but Ben could see the little girl was angry — angry at Turner . . . at the world . . . at fate . . . at herself. "I didn't use any soap on it."

But Turner wasn't listening. "You damned fool kid!"

Andy tried to parry that remark, but Turner raged on. "You've been nothing but trouble since we got you. Complaining about my food, complaining about your damned dirty hands. Saying your damned prayers. You'd be a sight less trouble with your throat laid opened wide and smiling."

The bowie knife flashed in the morning sunshine, and Andy's eyes expanded. She scrambled back and sat down in the cold stream as Turner went for her.

Ben lunged and tackled the knife arm.

Turner came around with a left, catching Ben just above the belt. Ben staggered, then dove again for the moving blade. His momentum carried them both into the shallow stream, scattering Andy's neatly arranged utensils.

The sting of the icy water crept into Ben's clothes and under his shirt. He kicked up a knee and lifted Turner over backward. The smaller man fell into deeper water. Ben pivoted, clinging to the knife hand, and pinning Turner's left arm under one knee. With his free hand, Ben grabbed Turner's throat and plunged his head under the water.

Wilson struggled against Ben's weight. His head broke water once. He gulped. And then he went under again.

Ben had no idea how long he held him down. His mind was busy overseeing the dozen or so different things that might cause a fight like this to take an ugly turn. But when the struggle went out of Turner, and the bowie slipped from his fingers, Ben heaved the sputtering man out of the icy currents and tossed him on shore.

Scott and Tom had showed up by this time, curious at the commotion going on. They dragged Turner up onto the grass and turned him onto his stomach to cough up the water he'd taken in.

Ben shagged the dripping water from his arms, breathing hard. He turned to Andy. "You all right?"

She nodded her head, shivering in her wet clothes in the cool morning air.

Ben pulled in two or three deep, settling breaths and said, "Let's find something dry to get you into."

"And you, too?"

"Me, too," he said, looking down at himself.

"But the dishes?" she protested, seeing them all scattered around.

"Later," he said, taking her by the arm.

Turner Wilson spent the rest of the morning splashing about in the stream until he found his knife. He sloshed back into camp as the others were packing the mule and making ready to leave. He hadn't eaten, and he probably wasn't hungry either, Ben thought, watching him over the curve of his saddle. Turner wasn't smiling, nor was he giving anyone a chance to catch his eye.

Andy had on a dry shirt Tom had lent her. Ben had resurrected a change of clothes from the bottom of his saddlebags that had already seen more than their fair share of sweat and dust.

Turner went about camp throwing his belongings into a canvas sack. He saddled his horse and swung aboard, still dripping. But the sun was high, and the morning warming, and it wouldn't be too long before he'd be dry again, and so would the clothes that Ben had draped over the pommel of his saddle.

Hallidae came up to Ben, leading his horse. "If we make decent time, we'll ride into Alpine this afternoon and look the place over."

"We can take Andy in with us and drop her off then," Ben said.

Hallidae shook his head. "No. She stays."

"We already talked about it, Neville. She's to be left the first place where she can be cared for. There is no good reason to leave her behind."

"If we drop the kid off tonight and then

we hit the bank in the morning, how long do you think it will be before your young friend there is down in the sheriff's office pointing out our pictures from his posters?"

Ben frowned and resumed work on the cinch, throwing a second loop through the buckle. "Anyplace we drop her off she'll be able to finger us. She's a bright kid. How long do you think it's going to take before she catches on what we are really about? Especially if she gets wind that there's something on the back of that mule other than Turner's cooking gear."

"Don't think I haven't been pondering that problem, Ben." Neville said it matter-of-fact, but Ben read something deeper in his words.

Ben glanced back at Andy. She was teasing a chipmunk with a scrap of bread. She smiled at him when she saw his look. The chipmunk got bold then. It dashed forward, took the bait from her fingers, scampered up over a rock, and sat there flicking his tail, devouring the food.

Andy came over, nearly stepping on the long tails of the shirt she wore, and said, "We have lots of chipmunks back home, Mr. Masters."

"So did we," Ben said. He lifted her onto his saddle and swung a leg over himself. "And back home is exactly where we need to get you now."

Eleven

Kelvin McKormick peered over the gold rims of his spectacles and seemed to be thinking of something profound to say. Kathleen felt prickles of perspiration break out and sting her neck beneath the high, brocade collar as she endured his long, piercing stare. It was as if his cold blue eyes were pointed icicles attempting to probe deep into her being. She wondered at first if the buttons of her green and gray dress were fastened in the wrong holes. She already felt culpable for shedding the black mourning dress so soon after George's death, but Marie had convinced her that in this new job such attire would not be appropriate.

McKormick had been less than enthusiastic during the interview the evening before. He'd listened while Marie had explained the situation to him, including the episode of the robbery. Afterward, as Kathleen and Marie stood in anxious silence, McKormick spoke of Marie's husband, praising Peter Winslick for his good business sense. For Peter's sake, and because business was good and men were scarce due to the almost hypnotic draw of the silver mines, he would consider hiring Peter's recently widowed sister-in-law to work behind the counter . . . on a trial basis.

Finally McKormick cleared his throat. His thick Scottish brogue rose to an imposing resonance. "I have never had a woman working behind my counters before, Mrs. Hamil. But I'm a fair man who believes a woman properly trained and looked after can handle a job such as this."

"Thank you for your confidence," Kathleen said, biting her tongue. *If only she didn't need the job so bad. . . .*

"Yes, of course." Kelvin McKormick lifted his chin and peered out across the stacked counters of dry goods, and up at the merchandise hanging from the rafters like last night's laundry. "Your brother-in-law, Peter, is a fine businessman, and I respect that," he went on, repeating almost word for word the speech he had given her the evening before. As he spoke, he strolled along the aisles, his hands clasped rigidly behind his back holding down the tails of his coat, his chin elevated.

The lord of the manor, she thought, following behind, knowing instinctively that this was the proper place for her inside the walls of McKormick's Mercantile and Assay.

"First ye must learn the location of every item on the shelves, and those that are kept in back. When a customer asks for an item, ye must be prompt in your reply."

"Yes, Mr. McKormick." *Me lord.*

He directed her to a booth built out from the back wall with an iron-grill window like a teller cage in a bank. A man with a green visor pushed up on his forehead smiled out at her from behind the bars. *A perfectly happy prisoner in Mr. McKormick's realm,* she thought.

"This is Mr. Reading — my assayer," he said.

"Morning, Miss —"

"*Mrs.* Hamil," McKormick corrected primly. He started off in another direction. "Down this aisle are the canned goods: coffee, beans, lard. Across from the groceries, we keep the kitchenware. Down this way are the shoes, and over on the next aisle is millinery."

McKormick strode along the aisles giving a precise litany of every item. He paused in front of a row of curved glass display cases to explain the watches, fountain pens, and revolvers arrayed there. "Of course, ye'll want Whithers" — Whithers being the other clerk that Kathleen had met the evening before — "nearby when ye show these items. He knows them well, and can help ye explain their intricacies to the customer."

"Certainly, Mr. McKormick."

He peered over his spectacles and added with great earnestness, "And ye'll want Whithers to watch over ye when ye count out the change. At least for the first few weeks until ye learn how."

"Certainly, sir." She strived not to allow her growing irritation to show.

After they had made the rounds, McKormick brought her to a shelf along the back wall. "And finally, we have the toys. For the wee ones, ye know. Pop guns, tops, spirals, dolls. Ye will find them all here. Now, have ye any questions before I place ye in Whithers' competent hands?"

Kathleen had plenty of questions, not the least being how Mrs. McKormick put up with such an insufferable man. But she needed the job, and she merely shook her head and said, "I believe I will learn quickly, especially with Mr. Whithers' assistance. We have, however, not discussed my compensation."

"Ah, the compensation." He smiled thinly at this, the first real look of pleasure she had seen on his otherwise gray, business-always face. "Well, now, lass, I normally start my clerks at sixty-five cents a day, paid weekly."

That sounded a proper compensation for having to work with a taskmaster like McKormick.

"However, considering that ye are a woman,

and considering ye will need extensive train-ing. And of course considering ye have not the obligations of a man, I believe forty-five cents a day is appropriate to start off with. And I will withhold the first two weeks' wages against any errors ye will make at the reg-ister." He smiled a genuine smile now. "How does that sound to ye, Mrs. Hamil?"

Kathleen choked on the anger that rose in her throat, and absolutely knew that the flames that leaped from her eyes would scorch every shred of gray hair off Kelvin McKormick's fuzzy muttonchops. But she needed the job. *Damn it!* She composed her-self, spoke sweetly — despising herself for her duplicity. "That will be adequate, Mr. McKormick."

Just the same, she had to look away when she said it.

The town of Alpine spread out beneath his spyglass like a miniature in a crystal globe. Ben shifted his view to one of the two tallest buildings, but could not identify it. For the most part, afternoon shadows enveloped the town, except where the failing light managed to catch and flash off the parapets of those few buildings that rose above the others.

"Let me see, Ben."

Ben passed the spyglass across.

"Busy little place, this town of Alpine," Neville said. He glanced up, shielding his eyes with the flat of his hand against the low, needle-sharp rays that pierced the ridge line far to the west.

This part of the Colorado Rockies resembled the hoed furrows of a corn field, rising and falling one after the other like waves. They had just spent the greater part of the day climbing and descending those furrows, which had brought them down to this spit of land above the town of Alpine, Colorado.

"It is too late to do any more today," Neville said finally. "By the time we ride down there it will be dark, the bank will be closed."

"But the saloons will still be open," Wilson said, snatching up the lens and checking the community below. He'd not mentioned the fight, rising up out of his depression around noon and easing back into his gratingly snide self. Ben had put the incident behind him, too.

They did not hear Andy coming up behind them until she said, "What are you looking at?"

Neville came about. "How long have you been standing there? I told you to wait with the horses."

"Mr. Deveraux is watching the horses. Is that where you do your banking, Mr. Hallidae?"

Neville gave Ben a glance.

"Neville has some money down there. He is going to make a withdrawal, but it is too late tonight to do so." Almost immediately Ben felt a pang of regret. Lying as such had never been much of a problem with him before, but he felt certain Andy had seen through the untruth now.

"Oh," she said and stepped over to a jutting rock, grabbed hold, and leaned out over the valley that dropped steeply away. "This makes me dizzy."

"Here, get back from there, Andy," McintyTe said. "You'll fall and bust your head."

"She can't fall, Fish Brain," Turner needled. "She is a little angel. Flies around like a bird on gossamer wings."

Neville said, "Go on back to Tom and stay put."

"You keep an eye on that nigger," Turner called after her. "You know how them people are."

Ben said, "One of these days Tom is going to have all he's going to take from you, Turner."

Turner grinned. "Hell, Spyglass, that nigger ain't got the guts to stand and fight." He stabbed the brass telescope into Ben's hands and went back to his horse.

Neville propped a boot up on a rock and

brushed at the day's accumulated dust. "I don't know what I'm gonna do with you boys, Ben. We ain't never been what you would call a happy family, but we ain't never had this scrapping all the time before, either."

Ben watched the valley filling up with the night. "What do you suggest, Neville?"

"I haven't yet decided." He strolled back to the horses.

Ben was aware of Scott's eyes jogging between Neville and himself. Scott gave him a weak grin that dimpled his fleshy cheeks, then shoved his hands deep into his pockets and made his way back to the horses. Scott was troubled, too, Ben could tell.

They'd been together most of three years. Made quite a reputation for themselves down around Socorro and Ruidoso. A reputation that followed them up through Santa Fe, and into the fresh-faced mining towns of Colorado. Maybe they'd been together too long.

Ben remembered the marshal that had tagged them up through New Mexico. An older fellow, big and bold, riding a tall horse that never seemed to tire. He didn't know what authority, if any, a Deputy United States Marshal would have outside the Territories, but he didn't figure that would throw up much of a challenge for a determined man — a man like Walter Devon.

Ben glanced at his companions unsaddling their animals and laying out camp for the night. Andy stood off to one side with that doll clutched under one arm, giving directions here and there to the men, who for the most part ignored her, or conceded for no other reasons than to avoid the debate they knew would follow.

For the first time, Ben Masters seriously questioned the wisdom of bringing the girl along. But what else could he have done?

He wasn't sure, and an idea that Neville had planted in his head that morning was beginning to put down roots.

Twelve

"Where is the water?"

"Probably a stream or a seep down below," Scott said.

Andy peered off into the lengthening shadows. "Down this way?"

Wilson grabbed up a pail and tossed it at Tom. "Cotton, go fetch the kid some water, so as she can wash her precious little hands."

"Go fetch it yourself, Turner."

"I'm getting dinner on," he pleaded innocently.

Neville Hallidae regarded the two of them impatiently. "You go along with her, Cotton."

"I don't want to."

"Someone's got to go. What's wrong? Your leg broke?"

Ben came back from the picket line where he'd been checking on the horses. They'd been worked hard, and he wanted to see that they had grass for the night, even if it was only the short, stiff variety that grew in these mountains. What they needed was tall Missouri grass. The kind Ben remembered cool and thick between his toes as a boy running across summer fields back home.

"The horses need water," he said, "I'll tag along with you, Tom. Andy, come along."

Tom hesitated. Then, with a shudder of his big frame, he tramped along after Ben, the water pail swinging angrily at his side. He didn't speak as they clumped down the slope where wide-spaced ponderosa pine and Douglas fir stood and brown grama grass rustled beneath their boots. He and Ben followed the slope toward a line of aspen trees that looked a promising place to find water.

"What's been troubling you, Tom?"

"You mean other than that bothersome mouth back there what don't know when to shut up?"

Ben grinned. "That's not what I mean. Turner's been a bitter dose since we started riding together. You've always managed to ignore him before. We all do. He rides Scott as much as he rides you. The only one he backs down from is Neville."

"He don't ride you, Ben."

"Not so much in the noticeable ways. But he does it. Turner Wilson is not the person I'm talking about."

Tom stopped and looked at him. "Just who is it you are talking about?"

Andy had come to a stop, too. Ben said, "You're younger than Tom and me. How about you skip on ahead of us and check if there is any water there. We'll be along directly."

"All right, Mr. Masters."

"And mind where you step," he called. "I don't want any twisted ankles or busted legs to have to mend."

"I'm always careful," she shot back.

"I'll just bet you are," Ben said, but only loud enough for Tom to hear.

"And she always tells the truth, too," Tom added with a glint of admiration in his dark eyes.

Ben didn't try to hold back his smile. "Someone raised that kid proper."

"Maybe some of it will rub off on us," Tom said as they started moving downhill again.

"Andy getting under your skin?"

Tom glanced at Ben, surprised. "She don't bother me none. She's got her ways, but even on her worst day that little kid is better company than *Master* Wilson."

Ben laughed. "But something about her bothers you."

Tom buried his fist in his pocket and gazed down the hill at the bounding girl a hundred feet ahead. "She got a pap, Ben."

"So?"

"So, he's gonna come lookin' for her," Tom went on, trying to sound reasonable, "and when he does, he's gonna find her with a bunch of bad men running from the law in most every state west of the Mississip'. And if that ain't bad 'nough, he's gonna find her with a man of color. You know what they do to a colored man what they figure been messin' with a white girl?"

"You've treated Andy fine."

"Tell that to her father, or the law if'n he brings 'em along. Hark on to my words, Ben, they see she's with a Negro, they'll go reachin' for a stout rope first and talk reasonable about it later."

"You're making too much of it. Andy's father will be so grateful someone looked after his kid for him that he won't be able to thank us — and you — enough."

Tom gave a short laugh. "That's the way a white man sees it. Folks ain't lookin' for an excuse to stretch a white neck."

Tom thought it over some then said, "Well, leastwise, if'n we hand her over to someone in Alpine, we'll be long gone before her pap shows up to claim her."

"We aren't taking Andy into Alpine."

Tom stared at Ben. "But that was the idea all along. We was goin' to drop her off at the first town we got to."

"Neville thinks Andy will finger us when we knock over the bank."

"What are we gonna do? Welcome her into

123

the brotherhood? Hand her a gun and point her in the direction of the nearest candy store? What the hell is Neville thinking, anyway! Forget about that damn bank, drop the kid off, and let's hightail it out of here! We got money — plenty already aback that mule. What's Neville after? Lordy, he'll have to get hisself a second mule if'n he don't ease up on his miser grip and let us spend some of what we already got!"

Ben had the same misgivings. He watched Andy disappear down a ravine that hid all but the tops of the Aspen trees growing below. It was late in the season and already pockets among the dark green of pine trees at the highest elevations were beginning to show splashes of red and yellow. It promised to be an early winter. One that Ben did not particularly want to spend on the move. Especially in this Colorado high country.

He thought about Utah and Nevada, both possible wintering grounds. But the decision would be Neville's — it was always Neville's decision. For some reason that nettled him now. They could not go back down into the Territories without drawing the attention of that determined deputy marshal, Devon. So, for a while at least, a pleasant winter in Santa Fe, strolling along the plaza, smelling the smoke of piñon wood cookfires, enjoying the colorful adobes with their red chilies dangling like Christmas ornaments from the corbels of the portals was out of the question.

It occurred to Ben there was another place. A place he hadn't thought about in years. . . .

Andy's head popped up above the ravine and she waved an arm at them. "Mr. Masters, Mr. Deveraux," she shouted. "There is water down here. Lots of water."

Tom looked over his shoulder at where they had come from. "Mighty long walk for a bucket of water," he commented dolefully.

"I'll want to bring the horses down before dark," Ben said, putting aside his thoughts for the moment.

Andy found an unused pot from among Turner's kit and convinced Tom to part with some of his hard-carried and heavily cursed water.

"What are you about now?" Turner carped when she appropriated a corner of his coals for her pot.

"I am heating water so that we can all wash our hands and faces before eating."

"Oh, you are? I'll have you know that I built this here fire. And I banked up the coals. And I'm using them to cook on. So that makes it my fire, and I don't want to share it."

"I carried in the wood," Tom noted casually from where he was wiping the carbon from the globe of a candle lantern. "That makes it part mine, too."

Mcintyre hunkered down by the fire and poured himself a cup of coffee. "Didn't you borrow a match from me to light this here fire?" he asked, straight-faced.

Turner rolled his eyes and said, "All right, kid. You can heat your pot of water. Only don't expect me to wash in it. I like being dirty." He stuck a finger in the boiling food pot and gritted his teeth against the pain just long enough to see Andy's look of disgust. Then he raced the finger to his mouth and sucked the heat from it, grinning around the digit in a satisfied manner.

"Childish," Andy said, turning her back on him.

"You're so big and grow'd up yourself, are you?"

"I don't stick my finger in boiling stew," she pointed out, regarding him briefly over her shoulder with an expression Ben figured was true sorrow for someone of limited capabilities.

"You haughty little brat."

"Cut it out, Turner," Ben said, stepping between them.

Wilson drew the bowie knife and grinned

up at Ben. "You name it, I'll cut it out. How 'bout we begin with that little gal's flapping tongue?"

"You're the one with the flapping tongue," Tom said.

Turner shot him a narrow look.

Hallidae said, "Do I have to nursemaid all of you? Turner, put that thing away."

Turner chuckled. "We was just having a little fun, weren't we?" He glanced around for support and found it decisively lacking.

Hallidae said to Ben, "You keep that kid in line. I won't be responsible for what happens to her."

Ben said, "It's getting pretty hot around here, Andy. I need to take these horses down to water. Why don't you come along and give me a hand?"

"All right." She gathered up Susie Meyers and looked at Turner. "I'm sorry I made you mad, Mr. Wilson." Holding the long shirttails off the ground so as not to trip on them, she followed Ben down to the picket line.

Thirteen

"Why is Mr. Wilson always angry?"

"Some people don't know how to be any other way," Ben said as he walked on ahead with the halter leads of the six animals in hand. He'd put Andy atop one of the long-legged horses, and she gripped a handful of mane in one hand while the other arm wrapped around the tattered rag doll. Her bare feet had begun to crack and bleed from the rough countryside. If she was to stay with them another day, Ben knew he'd have to find the child warm and stout clothes.

"Maybe it was the way he was raised. My papa says that children reflect the parents that raised them."

Ben looked over at her. "Your papa has a saying for most every occasion, doesn't he?"

She shrugged her shoulders. "I suppose so. Mama used to call him her 'old gray-headed philosopher.' I don't know exactly what that means because Papa doesn't have gray hair. He is only thirty-two years old. That isn't old enough for gray hair, is it, Mr. Masters?"

"I don't think it's the years that matter so much as the way a person lives them, Andy."

Ben took off his hat and ran his fingers through his coarse brown hair. "Look at me. I'm two years younger than your pa and already there are streaks of silver showing up."

Andy leaned forward. "There ain't much gray."

"Not yet. But it won't be long."

"Is that because of the life you've led, Mr. Masters?"

Ben settled his hat back in place. "Let's just say it could have been lived better."

"Mr. Masters?"

"Yes?"

"Have you ever told a lie?"

Ben stopped to consider her sitting there astride a horse that seemed too vast for her short legs. Her wide, pale eyes studied him as he pondered his next words. "I suppose so. Everyone tells lies. Haven't you?"

Andy shook her head and started to say that she hadn't, then she reconsidered. "I told a lie once. It made Mama and Papa sad when they found out. They said that God was sad, too, when I told lies. So I promised I would not tell another lie again."

"You have never told a lie since? Not even a little white lie?"

Andy shook her head emphatically.

"What if you had to tell a lie to help someone?"

"How can telling a lie help someone?"

"Suppose your papa broke the law and the sheriff came to your house to arrest him. Suppose your papa was hiding in the cellar. Would you tell that sheriff that he was down there, or would you tell him that your papa was away?"

"My papa would never break the law."

"Well, just pretend."

Andy frowned. "I guess I wouldn't say anything at all, then."

"If you didn't, the sheriff and his deputies would search the house and arrest your papa. Wouldn't you tell a lie to save his skin?"

When Andy didn't reply, Ben looked back and discovered her weeping again.

"Sorry, Andy. Didn't mean to ride you on it. I forget what you've been through."

Andy brushed away a tear. "My papa would never do anything wrong, and I will not lie." There was a finality to her words that told Ben the discussion was at an end.

Ben resumed his trek down to the stream. After what seemed an almost endless silence, Andy said, "Mr. Masters? Would you ever lie to me?"

Ben's heart solidified into a lump. He didn't look at her when he said, "Yes. If I figure I needed to."

"Mr. Masters?"

Ben kept his eye on the line of treetops that marked the waterway ahead. "What?"

"Mr. Hallidae doesn't really have any money in that bank down in Alpine — does he?"

Ben stopped and turned on the girl with a suddenness that set her back on the horse. "What made you say that?"

"Mr. Hallidae wants to steal from that bank, doesn't he?"

"Listen to me, Andy. Don't you ever let on to Neville what you just said. Understand me?"

"It's true, then."

Ben nodded his head. "It's true. But if Neville ever suspects you know, it will go badly for you."

"Is he a bad man?"

"Andy," Ben said with regret in his voice, "we are all bad men."

She shook her head. "You aren't a bad man, and neither is Mr. Deveraux, or Mr. Mcintyre."

"Yes we are, we're just different, that's all. But every one of us is a wanted man."

Andy swallowed and regarded him cautiously. "But you wouldn't hurt me?"

"No, I wouldn't. But Neville might."

Andy's face looked pink and washed-out in the evening light, and her eyes seemed to have grown wider and wiser. Her voice was weak when she spoke next, fighting down the emotion that closed its fist around her throat. "Mr. Masters? I'm scared. I want my papa."

Ben dropped the halter leads and took Andy into his arms. He couldn't help himself. Andy needed the release only crying could give, and in the growing twilight, he held her, and she sobbed bitterly into his shoulder.

Walt Devon kicked aside the sticks and dried grass scattered about the hard ground then lifted a stern face toward the tree line not so far above them now. It seemed to him that there was certainly more left to climb than they had already managed. But that was not what concerned him now.

Landy Peterman rode up from another direction.

Devon said, "Did you find any more for your collection?"

Landy looked grim. "I didn't find anything, Marshal. Didn't find any tracks at all."

Franklin Dean was scouring the ground with his eyes. "Men just don't up and disappear, Marshal," he said impatiently.

"Well, these five seemed to have," Devon said, stepping heavily into his stirrup and swinging a weary leg over the saddle. "We'll keep looking. They were heading west. Let's figure that is still where they are heading. What is west of here?" He stuck out a hand. Landy, by this time, was becoming adept at reading the marshal's thoughts. He pushed the tattered map into Devon's fingers.

Devon but glanced at the map. He'd already studied it thoroughly a dozen times, and almost at once returned it. There was the Continental Divide west of here — certainly not a likely destination for Neville Hallidae. And beyond that lay more than a dozen towns, sprung up in the last few years as suddenly as the desert flowers appear after the spring rains. The rains that watered these upstarts were colored silver and gold.

Stanley Hedstrom reined his horse over. "Marshal, this here valley runs pretty much up to the Divide. If I was Neville Hallidae, I'd probably follow it. It would make for easier riding than trying to tackle that peak straight on. The nearest pass is Cottonwood Pass, and it is a good piece out of our way to the south — a full day's ride, I'd guess."

"You figure Hallidae would take a valley like this one here up and over?"

"Yes, sir," Hedstrom said. "It would be the easiest way over. It'd offer a more gradual climb, except for just a little bit at the top."

"Well, deputy, if I was to make a guess at it, I'd say you were right. Hallidae would take the road of least resistance. It's what he's done most of his sorry life." Devon turned his gaze again upon the unfriendly granite peaks above them. "We, on the other hand, ought not to be tempted by Hallidae's deficiencies of character."

The momentary glow in Hedstrom's face faded as swiftly as the daylight was fading all around them, stamped out by Devon's words.

Devon pointed a finger at the rocky wall that stood before them. "We go that way."

"Why, Marshal?" The question came out in a burst.

"Because I say so," Devon came back. The flint left his eyes and he said patiently, "Have you looked at that map Landy carries around in his saddlebag?"

"Some." Hedstrom tried to disguise the hurt in his voice.

"All these valleys run mainly north and south. Sure, they'll take you up and over the top — eventually — but where we want to go is west. Let Hallidae take it the easy way. Let him linger an extra day in making the passage. We are already a day behind him, maybe more now that his trail has gone cold. We can make up that day by striking due west."

"I vote with the marshal," Franklin Dean said.

Devon rotated in his saddle and speared Andoreana's father with a narrow stare. "Don't cast your vote until this here posse becomes a democracy. And so far it hasn't."

Dean withered under Devon's gaze.

Devon returned his attention to Hedstrom. "I appreciate the observation. If you have any more to make, don't be shy about it." Devon turned his horse and got it moving slowly up the slope. He knew the men needed rest. Lord, he needed it too, but he'd come too far, had been on Hallidae's trail too long to lose him this way. So long as there remained daylight to see by, Marshal Walter Devon was determined to use it.

He could hear the others plodding along behind him and put the sound of them out of mind, turning his attention fully to the unyielding ground, and the rising land around them.

Like Franklin Dean had said, men just don't up and disappear. . . .

Fourteen

Andy bent over the fire and dragged the pot of steaming water off the coals. "May I borrow more water, Mr. Deveraux?" she asked, with the pail already poised over the pot of hot water.

"Sure, go ahead," Tom said, glancing from the book tilted toward the feeble light of a candle lantern.

Andy seasoned the hot water mildly with the cold, tested it with a finger, then added a splash more. "It's ready for washing," she announced, unwrapping the wedge of green soap Mcintyre had given her.

Wilson snarled and continued to ladle the night's fare into blue tin cups. But despite his protestations, they were now clean cups. Andy had seen to that, and Ben, Tom, and Scott had backed her up. Neville had stayed out of the argument, though Ben had the impression that Neville appreciated Andy's hand at the dishes, too.

The men took their turns with the soap. Turner stayed away, mumbling to himself about the condition of men who stoop so low as to accept the coddling of females. When

Andy insisted that they say grace, Neville drew the line and carried his meal away and occupied himself with eating while Andy said the blessing.

After supper she put on more wash water and set herself in charge of cleaning up the dishes. Turner howled when he discovered that she'd used up the last of the coffee water. Neville suggested that he tramp on down to the stream to fetch some more.

"Send Cotton," Turner came back.

"You're the one making all the noise," Neville said.

Andy sat beside Tom with Ben's blanket over her shoulders. "Mr. Deveraux can't get water now. I want him to read to me."

The surprise on Tom's face blossomed into a grin that he directed at Turner. "I'm reading to the chil'. You fetch the water this time."

Turner's fist balled, and his knuckles blanched.

Ben said, "A cup of coffee sounds mighty good right at the moment. When you come back, bring the horses with you. They've had time enough to eat and drink their fill by now."

Turner cast around a helping hand. Discovering only grins and chuckles, he resigned himself to the task, picked up the water pail, and disappeared into the night.

"Thanks, Andy."

"For what?" she asked, her eyes wide with innocence.

"For saying you wanted me to read to you. For helping old Tom out of another trip down to the stream. That's what for, chil'."

"But I do want you to read to me."

"You do?"

"Yes. I wouldn't tell a lie."

"No, of course not. All I got is this here book 'bout a boy named Huck and his colored friend, Jim, a runaway."

"What's a runaway?"

"Why, chil', that's a slave who decided he ain't gonna be a slave no more and takes matters into his own hands."

"Will you read it to me?"

"I can't finish it all in one sitting."

"That's all right." Her voice caught. "My mama used to read me whole books, a little bit at a time."

"She did?"

"Hu-huh."

Tom glanced over at Ben with genuine joy and pride.

"Well, I'll start over from the beginning and read to you 'bout that scoundrel Huck Finn, and Jim, and their adventures on the Mississip'." Tom flipped back to the first page and tilted the book into the candlelight.

Andy made herself comfortable beside him, huddling Susie Meyers close to her inside the blanket. "Now, you don't make any noise, Susie," she said to the doll, "and Mr. Deveraux will read to us all about a runaway."

Ben moved in a bit closer, too, as Tom's deep voice began the tale, and as he did so, something buried deep in his memory came to the surface. He was thinking of Rita again, and this time he did not wonder why, only where she might be and what she was doing at this very moment. And he seemed to remember something else, too: the long-forgotten sound of his mother's voice reading stories to the little girl so very much, in Ben's memories, like Andy.

Tom read twenty-eight pages before the cold drove them all to their blankets. Toward the end even Neville had perked up an ear, though he tried not to be obvious about it. But neither Ben nor Scott minded being obvious in their interest, and Turner was getting a kick out of the story too, adding his comments as Tom read along. Turner had definite plans for the prissy Widow Douglas, and he mentioned once or twice that Huck's pap sounded to be much like his own had been.

"Mr. Masters?"

"Why don't you just call me Ben?"

"My papa said I should never call a grown-up by their first name unless I put an *aunt* or an *uncle* in front of it."

"I give you permission to call this grown-up by his first name."

"And you can call this grown-up by his first name, too," Tom added as he picked up pine cones, tossed them in the fire, and smoothed the ground where he intended to lay out his bedroll.

"Why don't you just call all of us grown-ups by our first names? All this politeness gets on my nerves. Besides, *Mr. Wilson* is what everyone called my old man."

Andy gave it a try and was embarrassed. She said, "How about I call you Uncle? You can be Uncle Ben, you can be Uncle Tom —"

"Hold up there, chil'. You can call me Tom straight out, or you can call me Mr. Deveraux. But I will not be called Uncle Tom."

Andy was confused.

Turner laughed. "You appear a right fine Uncle Tom type, Cotton."

Andy looked to Ben. "I'll explain it to you later."

"Oh," she said. "It's one of *those* things. The kind of things kids aren't supposed to know."

Ben laughed. "It's not that at all. Now you lay down and let me tuck you in."

"Mr. Masters — I mean, Uncle Ben. Will you stay near me tonight?"

"I'll be right under that tree."

"I had a bad dream last night."

"You made mention of it this morning. Dreams won't hurt you."

"I know that," she said. "Only" — her voice dropped to a whisper — "I'm not sure it was a dream at all."

Her sudden intensity riveted Ben's attention. He lowered his voice to match hers. "What was the dream about?"

Andy hesitated, not certain how to continue. "I dreamt that there was a man looking at me. I could feel him leaning over me, just looking at me. I dreamt that he put his hand on top of me. I could almost even feel it through the blanket. But when I woke up all the way, I wasn't sure anymore."

She shrugged her shoulders. "It has gotten all hazy now. But it scared me so that I could not get back to sleep. That is why when first light came to the valley, I got up and went to work on Mr. Wilson's dishes. Whenever something troubled Mama, she'd commence to working twice as hard. She used to say work was medicine to the mind. So, I got up and went to work."

Ben gave Andy a reassuring smile. "It sounds to me like it was a bad dream after all. You know how real they can seem at times. Nobody here is going to hurt you. But if you have that dream again, you just give a shout and I'll be up lickety-split."

Andy smiled up at him, satisfied.

"Now, you get to sleep."

"Uncle Ben?"

"Yes?"

"Will you listen to my prayers?"

Ben grinned down at her sleepy face. "Go ahead and say them. I'll wait right here until you're finished."

"You have kids?"

Walt Devon had been occupied with his own private reflections when Franklin Dean spoke. Devon lifted his head where he sat in the cold shadows of a great granite boulder, huddled within his heavy wool coat. The yellow light of their fire — hard won at this elevation with its thin air and little dry kindling — moved across his rough face and set the crease in his worn brown hat glowing.

"I have one. A boy."

Franklin gave a short laugh and poked at their fire with a stick. "Kids can be a trial, can't they? You're mad as hell at them one minute, the next you're fretting like an old mother hen. Your boy, Marshal, what's his name?"

"Ferro."

"A family name?"

"His grandpa, on his mother's side."

"He must be a fine grown man by now."

"He's a grown man all right, but he didn't turn out like I'd hoped. I reckon I was always too busy when it counted." Devon tossed a pebble at the fire, lost for a moment in thought. "When kids grow up without a firm hand or without a mother to care for them, they sometimes go sour. Ferro did. He is in a Kansas jail right now. Been in and out of them more times than I care to count."

"Sorry, Marshal," Franklin said.

Devon went back to his thoughts.

Franklin Dean watched the fire awhile. There was emotion in his voice when he spoke again. "Andoreana is a fine young girl. No finer daughter could a man ever hope for, Marshal." Emotion got the better of him and he left the campsite in a hurry.

"Think we'll find his kid, Marshal?" Stanley Hedstrom asked.

Walt Devon nodded his head. "We'll find her if she is indeed with Neville Hallidae."

"You don't think she is?"

Devon looked at him sharply. "I didn't say that, deputy. She is as likely to be with

Hallidae as she isn't. But so far I've seen no sign of it."

"He seems pretty certain."

"He sees it through the eyes of a father that has just lost a wife and a son. That, deputy, is a man desperate not to lose any more than he already has."

Hedstrom went for more coffee and Devon returned to his thoughts, but they were more troubled than before. That always happened when he reflected on his son . . . and the woman who bore him only to die seven years later.

But that was many years ago. Time worked its salve into Walter Devon's wounds. He glanced out into the darkness where Franklin Dean had disappeared.

Franklin's wounds had only just begun to ache. . . .

Fifteen

Ben Masters shivered in his buttoned-up coat and leaned closer to the low fire to warm his hands. Andy was asleep, and so were Neville, Turner, and Scott. Tom still turned restlessly in his blankets. Ben considered building up the fire, but that would only prolong his own insomnia. Sleep was not coming easy this night. He glanced at the small bundle curled up under his blanket, and pondered the dream Andy had told him about. Ben glanced around the dark campsite, his view lingering briefly on each of the sleeping men curled tightly in their blankets against the night's chill.

"No," he told himself firmly.

"No, what?" said a deep voice, low enough not to wake the others.

Ben was surprised to find Tom standing over him with a blanket wrapped around his shoulders.

"You talking to yourself now, Ben?" Tom said, hunkering down near the red coals.

"I guess I was." Ben watched the embers brighten in the slight breeze. "Can't sleep?"

"No more than you, it seems."

Ben rubbed his arms to stir the blood.

"Winter is coming on. I feel it already. Another month and these mountains will be snowed in."

"Sure ain't like Georgia."

"Or Missouri," Ben said.

"Do I detect a note of homesickness?"

Ben looked over and frowned. "I'm thirty years old!"

"That ain't too old."

Ben thought a moment. "No, not homesick. But I am getting a little tired of always being on the move. Always looking over my shoulder wondering when the next lawman will show up, or if the next person I meet might remember my face from a poster somewhere." He laughed softly. "And I am for certain getting tired of sleeping on hard ground, eating Wilson's grub, and spending most every night either cold or wet."

Ben grinned then. "Maybe I am getting just a little homesick. I've been away ten years, and I've been wondering about my family."

"Because of Andy?"

"Partly. It began the morning we knocked over the bank in Buena Vista. The next day we picked up Andy. Maybe it's time to go back to Missouri. Maybe they need me. I don't know. Sounds crazy, doesn't it?"

But Tom wasn't laughing, or even smiling. His black face, nearly disappearing against the curtain of night, was pinched with concern, and his eyes showed big and white. "It ain't crazy, Ben. Them things happen all the time. People sometimes know things that they shouldn't be able to. I don't know how. Old men read the hairballs, or chicken bones spread out, or even small stones shook in a blind woman's hand and tossed out onto the ground. Sometimes it's just a feeling that won't go away. The week before they sold my mam and sister, my pap couldn't sleep a wink, no sir. And he moaned all the day long that something bad was gonna happen, only he didn't know what. Then the Man in the big house come and take his wife and daughter away to the auction block."

Ben grimaced. "Nothing you could have done to stop him from taking them?"

"Sheee-it, Ben, niggers have no say when the Man gets it in his head to do such and that."

Ben watched a flame struggle up from the coals, then die back into the bed of embers. A chill wind brightened them. He said, "Tom, Andy knows about us. Who we are, what we do."

The big black man seemed unaffected. "I ain't surprised. She's a bright little girl, even though she has her ways about her. I'm surprised that she didn't figure it out right off."

Ben nodded his head toward one of the sleeping forms. "If he finds out, it could mean trouble. And if it comes to that kind of trouble, well, I guess it will be me going against him — and everyone else."

"Almost everyone else," Tom said, watching the embers.

Ben glanced over and gave Tom a grin. "I was hoping you'd back me."

Tom huffed. "I must be getting old, Ben. Was a time when I'd help no white man, unless it helped me too."

They sat in the quiet of the night staring at the dull red glow in the fire pit. In the distance, two bull elks called to each other across the dark mountains. Finally, Tom stood and said, "I think I'll give sleep another try."

"Night," Ben said softly. He sat by the fire awhile longer, watching the red remains of their fire wink out one coal at a time. Then he, too, moved wearily over to the place he'd cleared earlier by the dark Douglas fir. He eased himself down on his saddle blanket, leaned against the tree, and huddled deep into his coat.

But although his eyes closed, Ben's brain remained wide awake, and that night his ears heard everything.

The next morning Ben and Neville rode

down into Alpine for a look at the bank. Tom had asked Ben to pick him up some tobacco while he was in town; Turner said they needed more beans. Ben jotted it all down in the borders of a page of the *Chaffee County Times* that Tom had picked up in Buena Vista.

When they rode out of camp, it was with a growing sense of misgiving that made Ben glance over his shoulder at Tom. He regarded Andy with a long, troubled stare. Then the trees closed in behind him and it was only he and Neville, moving quietly along the steep game trail winding down the mountainside.

Ben wrestled with a troubled spirit as they made their way toward Alpine. Maybe it was simply the tension of sizing up the next job, or maybe it was leaving Andy behind and away from his watchful eye . . . or maybe he was only tired from a sleepless night.

Why had he bothered to stay awake, anyway? Because of Andy's dream? The kid was getting to him. He had to be cautious, he warned himself, or he'd weaken and allow the girl to crawl too deeply under his skin.

But by the time he and Neville had come among the dry-timber shacks outskirting the high, windswept town of Alpine, Ben had arrived at one conclusion. He did not want to take this bank today — or any other day. Yet, he'd come too far with Neville Hallidae to turn and cut now. Too many years for a simple and easy "goodbye."

They turned in at a hitch rail in front of a whitewashed building shoehorned between two others. Alpine did not look to be a very substantial place and, for some reason, Ben thought of a pile of dry kindling as he wrapped his reins around the post.

The building they had tied up at was called Purdy's Wet Goods. Ben turned his eyes up the crooked street where the clapboard emblems of commerce leaned and staggered, thrown up along the crippled street almost as if an afterthought.

If Alpine was going to be one of those towns that survived the test of time, certainly no one here believed it yet. But, from the number of buildings, Ben could see there were plenty who were there for the moment. There were only two structures of any substance that Ben could see — both hotels.

"This place have a bank?" Ben asked as Neville came around his horse, shedding his coat in the late morning warmth.

"It's got a bank, and from what I picked up in Buena Vista, it ought to be packed solid with the dollars that the mining companies have converted from scrip."

"Then maybe it's too heavily guarded." Ben immediately regretted his words — or was it the tone in his voice that drew Neville's wary glance?

Neville nodded his head up the street. "Let's take a look at this place."

Alpine was a mixture of wooden sidewalks and no sidewalks at all. Flimsy bare-board shacks and sheds stood shoulder-to-shoulder with a less abundant variety of more substantial wooden buildings. Several even wore a thin covering of paint. In a few places, canvas tents flapped in the high-mountain wind — some sporting gaudy false fronts. *There were always the optimists,* Ben mused. A few more permanent-looking places stood out. The hotels were among these, erected upon formidable rock foundations. An occasional building here and there was even constructed entirely of the rocks of the area. But for the most part, Alpine was a colorless place with a temporary look about it, and Ben had the notion that one day the wind would blow it all down the side of the mountain.

Despite its flung-together appearance, Alpine was unmistakably a place bustling with the commerce of mining. Buckboards and wagons flowed through the crooked street like water in a stream overburdened with rocks. Some came empty; others loaded down to the axle beams with boxes and barrels. Some bared their cargo to the wide, blue sky; others hid it beneath sheets of canvas.

They came and went like large mats of up-rooted vegetation caught in the currents. A few mules made their way with the jetsam, and even fewer horses that were not harnessed to some sort of wheeled conveyance. The air was heavy with the stink of manure, and the rumble and rattle of people on the move.

Ben dodged the oncoming commerce while trying to read the shingles that grew out of the buildings with little regard to visibility or head clearance: RIGNALD'S POST AND COMPANY . . . HERRMANN & LIEBER WHOLESALE LIQUOR DEALERS . . . BERTIE'S DRY GOODS . . . THE COLORADO STORE . . . DENTIST . . . DRUG STORE . . . YELLOW BIRD SALOON . . . ST. LOUIS LAGER BEER . . . and on and on, until Ben was nearly dizzy trying to decipher them all. In the space of two blocks he counted eighteen dealers in liquor, four dry goods stores, a German bakery, two barber shops, two undertaking parlors, four assay offices, and an uncounted number of mining supply and hardware stores. And there were others, too.

And then he spied what he was looking for, across the street and tucked in between a building that sold shingles and a narrow newspaper office painted green.

BANK.

152

The sign stood out farther, and was bigger than the rest of the signs nearby.

Ben nudged Neville and pointed. Neville had been eyeing the dark interior of a saloon over the batwing doors.

"Busy place, this town of Alpine."

Ben nodded his head. "Looks like a man could turn a dollar or two here."

Neville grinned, then jabbed a thumb over his shoulder at the saloon. "After we're done inspecting where the folks in this busy place keep their money, I'm going to visit one of the watering holes. Maybe find some female company." He grinned.

Ben patted his vest pocket. "I got a shopping list to fill, but afterward, I'll lift a bottle with you, Neville."

"For old times' sake?"

Ben glanced at his partner. There was that wary tautness in Neville's face again. "Yeah, for old times' sake," Ben said.

They stepped off the tilting sidewalk and dodged the traffic as they made their way across the glutted street toward the bank.

Sixteen

Harlan Geckhorn had it all.

Well, almost.

Harlan had a good job. He had respect, authority, and a comfortable, although not a great, income. He was reasonably good-looking — Harlan sucked in his stomach and felt his pants slip down a notch — still young enough to get up in the morning without pain, and old enough to know his own mind. Harlan appreciated where he was going in life. He thanked God every morning that he did not have to crawl down into the dirty, dusty mines to make a living.

Yes, he had it all — well, almost — he thought as he strolled purposefully up the main street of Pitkin, savoring the clean mountain air. The morning sun was upon his back, pushing his shadow out ahead of him until it almost reached to the door of McKormick's Mercantile and Assay.

As far as Harlan Geckhorn could tell, he needed only one thing more in life, and then he *would* have it all! Unconsciously, he removed his hat and brushed back his thinning hair. He set the hat carefully back in place, adjusting it just right in the window of Tanner's Hardware Store as he strolled past.

Ahead, the door to McKormick's Mercantile loomed nearer. Geckhorn felt a tightness swell his throat. He smiled and nodded his head at two passing ladies and quickly riveted his view back on the doorway. His steps grew heavy. But he pressed on until he was there.

Harlan peered through the window, dragged his damp palms down his vest, and squared his shoulders. Yes, there was only one thing that Harlan Geckhorn needed now.

A wife!

And with a surge of determination, he gripped the brass door handle and stepped inside.

She heard the summoning ring of the bell that hung above the door, but Kathleen Hamil could not tend to it now, not with Kelvin McKormick frowning over her.

"Mr. Whithers will see to it," McKormick said, catching the clerk's eye and nodding toward the door that closed with a second insistent jangle.

Whithers abandoned the pickle barrel he had been muscling across the floor and McKormick returned his shriveling stare back at Kathleen Hamil. "I know this is but your second day behind the counter," he continued sternly, "but I must admonish that ye take more care with the receipts."

"I am very careful," Kathleen said in her defense, but McKormick's glowering face, frozen in its muttonchop frame, told her that he was not prepared to hear any excuse.

"Yet the receipts came up thirty-five cents short last night!"

"But I —"

McKormick held up his hand, cutting her words short. "This will come out of your salary, of course."

"Of course," she said, fuming inside at her submissiveness to this insufferable man.

McKormick pushed his spectacles up the bridge of his nose with the point of his long index finger and went on. "I admonish ye to take care, Mrs. Hamil. I have given ye an opportunity at this position out of pity for your wretched circumstances. But I can not abide carelessness."

"Yes, sir," she said, tasting bile.

"Very well, then. That said, I shall not harp on the matter further. Ye may return to your work now."

"Mr. McKormick," she said, "I was not the only person to take in money or give out change. Mr. Whithers did so, too, and if I may be so bold as to point out, so did you."

McKormick peered at her over the top of

his spectacles. "Do not be impudent, Mrs. Hamil. Mr. Whithers has an impeccable history with the firm. And I do not make errors where the finances of my business are concerned. Now, back to work with ye."

Kathleen Hamil ground her teeth, and over the roar of anger in her ears, she was aware of another voice speaking across the room. The voice was high, and it warbled uncertainly, as if the speaker behind it was not being one hundred percent candid.

"No, no, Whithers," it was saying, "I do not need a thing. Really. I was only just making my rounds and thought I'd step in and check that everything was all right."

Kathleen got a grip on herself. She touched her hair in place, and fixed a pleasant smile upon her face.

The owner of the voice was a man of medium height, bordering on the hefty side. He wore a black round hat with a narrow brim, gray pants held up with blue suspenders, and a gray wool vest — open in deference to the morning's warmth — over a white shirt with no collar. The man was looking about as he spoke, and making uncertain progress across the floor in her general direction.

McKormick peered up at him from the cash drawer and said, "Ye have never stopped in to check on things before, Sheriff Geckhorn."

Kathleen caught a glimpse of something bright pinned to his shirt beneath the vest just then.

Geckhorn stammered and laughed. "Well, you know it never hurts to keep tabs on what's going on."

McKormick looked skeptical. "I do not suppose that this visit has anything to do with the elections coming up this winter, does it, Sheriff?"

Harlan Geckhorn looked stunned. He waved a hand as if shooing away a swarm of gnats and laughed. "Absolutely not, McKormick. It's my duty, that's all."

Then Harlan caught Kathleen's eye and he smiled a funny wide grin. Kathleen thought the grin a little like that of the cat in *Alice's Adventures in Wonderland*. He swept his hat off his head and stepped over.

"And you must be the new wid— err — lady in town from Buena Vista?"

"I am Mrs. Hamil."

The grin widened. "I'm, er, I'm the sheriff of Pitkin. Harlan Geckhorn." He crammed his hat under his arm and stuck out a hand.

"It is nice to meet you, Sheriff," Kathleen said. She took his nervous hand, then wiped the moistness from her palm surreptitiously on the back of her dress.

"I heard you were just in." His face flushed

and he covered over his boldness with a chuckle. "You know how news travels in a small town. The sheriff is usually the first to get wind when someone new arrives." He glanced at McKormick. *Looking for corroboration,* Kathleen thought. But the old penny pincher was busy digging through his money drawer. *What else?*

"I'm sure you do," Kathleen said.

"Well . . . ah . . . well, I'm always around if you should need anything."

"Thank you. I shall remember that — if I should ever need anything."

"I'm . . . I'm practically right across the street." He grinned affably.

Kathleen smiled back at him gracefully.

Geckhorn stammered and pointed at the window. "Just over there. Says 'Sheriff's Office' right across the front."

Kathleen nodded her head. What more did he want from her?

Geckhorn put his hat back on his head. "Well, ought to be going, I suppose. Got a whole town to watch over."

He paused as if waiting for a reply.

"Well, see you all later," he said, casting his glance around the room. No one seemed particularly interested. He backed into a counter, stumbled, turned again to grin at her, then made his way out the door into the bright morning light.

When Geckhorn had gone, Kathleen discovered McKormick staring at her oddly. She forgot about the sheriff at once and wheeled brusquely back to her task of dusting the tops of baking soda tins around the corner of the far aisle . . . out of McKormick's view. A most pleasant place to be.

Straddling a fallen tree, Turner Wilson drew the edge of his bowie knife smoothly over the fine-grit whetstone he'd set up on the crumbling bark. And as he drew the blade across the stone, his view was not upon his work but upon the little girl sitting beyond their cookfire. She was talking to that doll again, and that irritated Wilson.

Turner glanced at Mcintyre, who was working bear grease into the seams of his boots, and his frown transformed itself into a smirk. *Fish Brain will be no trouble.*

He looked around for Tom. The black man had left the camp earlier. *Where the hell had that nigger gotten off to?* Turner studied the edge of their camp where the cliff fell away to the valley below. The faint odor of cigarette smoke coming from beyond it told him exactly where the ex-slave was. *Probably found a ledge to sit on and read. Damn niggers never do a lick of decent work unless you ride the hell out of them.*

Wilson turned his leering eye back to Andy. How she carried on with that doll. A piece of rag and cotton stuffing, that was all. Turner grinned. He could give her something much more interesting to carry on with. And as his brain dwelled on the possibilities, he grew more irritated that the other two men were near. And as his irritation grew, his knife sharpening became more energetic and less precise until he was fairly slapping the stone with the steel.

In anger, he knocked aside the whetstone and flung the knife away, driving the point of it deep into the trunk of a nearby tree. He stood glaring about the camp.

Scott stopped what he was doing and watched him curiously.

"What the hell you looking at, Fish Brain?"

"Nothing," Mcintyre said timorously, and went back to stuffing the seams of his boots with grease.

Mcintyre would be no trouble. But the nigger — he was another problem. Wilson began working on a plan to get him out of the way — at least long enough for what he had in mind.

Seventeen

Ben's lean frame cast a shortening shadow in the late-morning light as he and Neville dodged the swarms of wagons that filled the main street of Alpine, Colorado, and bounded up onto the sidewalk in front of the bank. Ben looked over his shoulder at the street they had just crossed, wondering where so many people went to after dark. This little hamlet seemed hardly large enough to contain them all. Back to a thousand leaning shacks thrown up next to a thousand little holes dug into the landscape. All in search of the precious color — the black sand with its yellow flecks of gold, the blue rock of silver.

All at once, he relished the lonely quiet of the mountains, away from the boomtowns that most assuredly went bust in a year or two.

Neville tugged Ben's sleeve, nodding at the doorway. They stepped inside where the scene shifted entirely. Neville stepped up to a quiet counter and made himself look busy with a steel pen and a bank deposit slip. Ben slouched against the table as if waiting for his friend — all the while carefully studying the layout. Now would be the time for throngs of people to keep the attention of the teller. But here the crowds had vanished. Ben felt conspicuous taking in the details of the windows, the iron-bar shutters, the great iron cage in which the teller stood. Embedded into a stone wall at the teller's back was a smallish vault perhaps four feet tall. Its heavy doors were open wide against the wall, revealing a second door behind — closed, but with the lever raised in the unlocked position.

Once earned, where did all the prosperity go? Certainly not into this bank. Neville had said the mining companies kept their money here, that the wealth of Alpine was in the pockets of those companies, and very little of it with the men who blasted the holes or carried off the rubble.

The floor beneath Ben's boots was solid pine, newly sawn, but already looking shabby. The cage in which the teller worked wore a fresh coat of gray paint. The door to the outside was a single wide panel with gilded glass and a small iron doorknob that looked glaringly out of place. There were iron brackets for a heavy bar to slide through too, but at present, the bar was missing.

Only one guard leaned against the wall, and he seemed more interested in what was going on in the street beyond one of the windows than by anything happening inside the bank.

163

That was understandable, Ben thought. Other than Neville and himself, and a single, sleepy-eyed teller thumbing through a file of small rectangular cards in a cardboard box, absolutely nothing was going on.

The door opened and Ben straightened up out of his slouch. A man stepped through and snatched up a pen from the inkwell at Neville's side. He scribbled in some numbers and took the slip of paper to the window. The teller dove into the cardboard box, riffled through the cards, selected one, compared it to the slip in his fingers, then opened a drawer and counted a wad of bills into the man's hand.

"Seen enough?" Neville said softly without looking over.

Ben nodded. "Not much to see."

The man at the window took his money from the teller and left.

Neville looked around the narrow building, taking in the details and committing them to memory. "Seen one, seen 'em all," he commented under his breath. Then louder, "I reckon I changed my mind, Ben. How 'bout we find us a bar somewhere to spend this here money at?"

"Whatever you say. It's your money."

How many times had he and Neville exchanged those words? Ben lost track. It was most always the same routine, ending with

Neville wadding up the deposit slip and tossing it into a pail as they left.

"That cracker box shouldn't be any problem," Neville said as they made their way along the busy sidewalk. "One guard and a teller that won't put up a fuss. A door to the back — an office? Maybe a way outside."

The sidewalk ended for a stretch of half a dozen buildings and then resumed beyond, like a missing tooth in an otherwise unbroken row. Only here in Alpine, teeth were missing at fairly regular intervals. They climbed back to the sidewalk when it again became part of the storefronts, and Ben said, "The bank looks easy enough. It's getting out of town afterward that's got me concerned." Actually, many things concerned Ben, not the least being his sudden and unexplainable desire not to rob the bank at all.

Neville grunted. "That will take a bit of planning, what with all these people milling around. It's still morning. Maybe the traffic thins out later on." Then he laughed and said, "If it thins out any more inside that bank, they'll close it down."

Ben and Neville chanced fate again, dodging the traffic to get to the other side where their horses were tied.

PURDY'S WET GOODS.

Neville lifted his chin to the yellow-and-green sign and said, "Reckon there's a decent bar in this place?"

"Judging by all the competition in town for the drinking dollar, I'd wager it's right up there with the rest of them," Ben fished the folded sheet of newsprint from his pocket. "You going to give it a try?"

Neville shrugged his shoulders and looked around. "Why not? No reason to butt heads with all these people just to get to a place to buy a drink, when there's a watering hole not three steps away. Anyway, I won't have so far to stumble afterward with our animals right outside."

Ben grinned. "Kind of early."

"Never too early for a drink, Ben."

"I got me some shopping to do first. I'll be around to join you when I'm done."

Neville pushed his hat onto the back of his head and regarded the doorway a moment. "Later we'll see what this boomtown looks like at closing time."

Ben lingered after Neville had disappeared inside, studying the signs up and down the street. A few doors down, the big round face of a clock on a shingle protruded out over the sidewalk.

Eleven thirty-two.

Ben spied a general store, and set his feet in its direction.

★ ★ ★

"You got a better idea, speak it now, Dean. If not, keep your complaints to yourself."

Franklin Dean shut his mouth and regarded Devon angrily. But the fire that had come to his eyes so quickly now died back. "I don't have any better ideas. It's just that I'm —"

"We know," Landy said, nudging his horse up alongside Andoreana's father. "You're worried for your little girl. But the marshal, and Stanley, and me, we're working it the best we know how."

"Damn rocks. Can't hardly follow a leaky bucket of paint across ground like this," Devon said, letting his own frustration get the better of him.

"There are always signs," Franklin Dean said. "You just got to know how to look for them."

Walt Devon swung around in his saddle and narrowed an eye at the troubled man. "Well, thank you for that insightful bit of information." He waved his arm grandly ahead. "Care to take the lead?"

"Just trying to help, Marshal."

Devon frowned, then let go of a heavy breath, and drew rein on his own anger. It wasn't Dean's fault. Devon was irritated at himself, at losing Neville Hallidae's trace. He had trailed the outlaw all the way up from

167

the Territories, and now to lose him like this, so close, galled the old marshal. "Sorry, Dean. I didn't have to jump all over you like that."

Stanley Hedstrom said, "It's plain we aren't gonna pick up Hallidae's trail unless we come up with a plan of some sort. You know, some kind of a system."

Devon settled his narrowed eye upon the deputy, but when he spoke, it was not in anger, but impatience. "What do you think we've been doing the last five hours?"

Stanley shrugged his shoulders and hesitantly offered, "Riding in circles?"

Devon nodded his head. "That's right, Hedstrom. Riding in circles." Devon turned his animal back upon the ever-growing spiral he was following. On one of these passes, on the leg of one of the ever-expanding sweeps, he was going to cross Neville Hallidae's trail, and when he did, Walt Devon would have his man. By all that was holy, he'd have his man!

Ben bought Tom a pack of Genuine Blackwell Bull Durham smoking tobacco with papers, a block of matches for camp use, four cans of Van Camp's, flour, baking powder, and a jar of prepared mustard for Turner. Scott got a plug of tobacco, and Ben bought a handful of long nines for himself.

Upon a shelf of ready-mades he located a pair of Jefferson shoes cut for a child and about the right size, according to Ben's estimation. He pondered over them at length, knowing that Andy would probably disapprove, but she had little say-so in the matter, and they were sturdy. On top of the growing stack in his arms he tossed a child-size red flannel shirt, cotton stockings, a pair of yellowish-brown nankeen trousers that would require the legs rolled up, and a pair of suspenders to keep them from sliding off her straight waist.

He considered the expense of a second wool blanket. Recalling the cold mountain nights, Ben decided three bits wasn't too high a price to pay and heaved one onto his arms. He carried the whole lot to the counter and tossed a bar of White Rose Glycerine Soap on top. He asked for two pennies' worth of mixed candy from the jars along a back shelf. Then he spied a blue wool hat marked size 1 — probably quartermaster's surplus from some outpost, but he added it to the pile.

The clerk tallied it all up and put it into a washed flour sack that cost Ben another penny, but the sack would be useful later, and easier to tie to his saddle than a brown paper wrapper.

He slung it to his shoulder and went back outside. It was one-fifteen by the large round clock face when Ben lashed the sack to his saddle and stepped through the door into the darkened interior of Purdy's Wet Goods.

He spied Neville leaning an elbow on the bar, sipping a beer. There were other men around, sampling Purdy's wet goods, talking among themselves. Miners mostly, it seemed.

"Darlene," he heard one of them call, "set 'em up again."

A tall woman — attractive, Ben thought — came through the back door and said, "Be with you in a minute, Sully."

Ben eased up next to Neville.

"She's a good looker, that one," Neville said.

Ben glanced at the woman. "She's spoken for, Neville. She got a ring on."

He laughed. "Rings don't mean anything to some women. Get everything you went after?"

"Hu-huh."

Darlene hauled a fistful of mugs over and passed them around to Sully and his friends. She turned to Ben. "What can I get you?"

"Beer."

She turned to a barrel on the back counter.

"Good beer?" Ben asked Neville.

"Passable," Neville said. "It's cold. Can't complain when you find someplace got cold beer."

Out back a door slammed and a towheaded man in his early forties came in, double-handing a wooden bucket that he heaved with a grunt and dumped inside an insulated box.

"There you go, Darlene," he said, glancing around at the paying customers. A grin lightened his face when he saw that their number had grown. He wiped his hands on the front of his overalls and disappeared out back again.

Darlene brought over Ben's beer and collected his nickel.

"How about we go somewhere, darling? Just you and me," Neville said.

The woman gave him a smile. "Not today, fellow. The mister's home, don't you know," she said, playing along.

Neville laughed.

At the far end of the dimly lit room, a man in a miner's shirt, a tattered bowler hat on his head, heaved himself away from the bar. With his beer in hand, and a crooked gait to his steps, he came toward Neville.

Eighteen

She tried steeling herself against the thoughts that brought tears so swiftly to her eyes. Tried to tell her troubles to Susie Meyers. Yet something was changing there, too. The solace she had found only a week ago in her cotton-stuffed friend was missing now. So much was missing in her life. So much pain had flooded in to replace it. Her whole world had jumped track and the new course it had taken altered everything.

And she did not understand the queasy sensation she got in the middle of her stomach whenever Turner Wilson looked at her, either. . . .

Andoreana glanced at him now, then quickly averted her eyes. He was still watching her.

She pulled her bare feet under the ragged hem of her nightgown, oddly self-conscious.

"Don't cry, Susie Meyers," she said to the doll, turning her back on Wilson and discovering the friendly face of Tom Deveraux smiling at her as he came into camp. Andoreana sat the doll upon a boulder. "Mr. — I mean, Uncle Ben, and Mr. Deveraux will take care of you and me until Papa comes for us."

"Where have you been, Cotton? Taking your midmorning *siesta?*"

Wilson's voice grated along Andoreana's spine like nails across a chalkboard.

Deveraux shot him a narrow stare. "I was thinkin'," he replied, lowering himself cross-legged upon the ground and beginning to rummage through his knapsack.

Wilson laughed. "That must have been a new experience."

Andoreana wondered why Tom put up with Wilson's badgering. She couldn't imagine the big man being afraid of Wilson, yet Tom endured the torment with the patience of an angel. All the while he kept a lid on the quiet rage that seemed to seethe eternally just below the surface. She could not have imagined her father, as gentle as he was, putting up with the kind of bedeviling Wilson dished out with scant regard.

Wilson stood by the fire, a shovel in his hand and a curious grin upon his face. Andoreana felt odd in the stomach as his view settled upon her again. A funny look came to his eyes.

"I'm going to make bread tonight, Cotton. I need you to run down and fetch me some more water."

"Fetch it you'self," Deveraux said, his attention on the contents of the rucksack that he was extracting and stacking in a pile upon the ground. Not finding what he wanted, Tom cursed softly to himself and returned everything unceremoniously to the leather war bag.

Wilson eyed Andoreana again, but when he spoke, it was to the black man. "I'm busy, Tom," he said, spreading butter over his words. "I'd appreciate you getting it while I dig a pit to bake bread in. We ain't had fresh bread in over a week. I've been saving the last of the flour. Now that Ben is bringing more back with him, I'll use up what I have."

"I said, I'm busy."

Wilson frowned, scratched an itch behind his right ear. He seemed to be concentrating on something, but Andoreana didn't care to observe him close enough to figure out what it might be. She looked back at Susie Meyers, and her lips dipped down into a frown, too. The never-distant sting of tears returned to her eyes. She shivered, not knowing why, for it was not cold this late in the morning. Yet her spine quivered as if a bug had crawled up it, and even more than before — if that was possible — she longed to see her father ride into view. Longed for him to leap off his horse and throw his arms around her and never ever let go.

174

* * *

When he came across the room, Ben could see that the man wasn't walking so almighty straight. He gripped his beer mug as if trying doubly hard not to spill any of it. He shouldered up next to Neville, banging the mug down on the bar, sloshing some over the rim.

Neville gave him a sidelong glance and opened the distance between them.

The man looked Neville up and down. "I ain't never seen you in here before, mister."

Ben sipped his beer and, over the rim of the mug, eyed the company at the end of the bar, who had been drinking with this fellow. They were talking low among themselves. These four had the look of hard-rock miners. Their frames were taut and lean, and solid muscle bulged the sleeves of their shirts from swinging a pick all day. But there was not a gun in sight among them, and right at the moment they seemed more embarrassed at their friend's brash actions than hostile.

Neville said, "Not surprising, since I ain't never been in here before. Not likely I'll ever be back, either."

"Is that so?" the man replied sardonically, rocking back slightly on his heels.

One of the miners at the end of the bar said, "Hey, Sully, come on back here."

Sully ignored them. "I seen the way you

looked at Darlene . . ."

So, that was it, Ben thought, grinning into his beer.

". . . heard what you said."

"You married to her, mister?" Neville shifted around to face the fellow.

"No . . ."

"Then it's none of your affair." He turned back to his beer.

"Darlene is kin of mine. Married to my kid brother. We don't take kindly to disrespect toward our women here in Alpine."

About that time the lady in question stuck her head around the doorway and said, "Sully, don't you go starting trouble in here again or I'll have Jabez haul you on home and show Martha what a miserable sot she's married to."

Sully's stare remained fixed upon Neville. He was a big man, worked into shape by moving mountains — one rock at a time, and at the moment too drunk to be reasoned with.

Neville, too, had had a couple more beers than he needed. Never a patient man when sober, Neville Hallidae was even less inclined now to let this affront pass. He was not as big as Sully, but Ben had tangled with Neville a time or two, and he knew the man was quick of feet and fists, and not likely to let pain stop him once he set his mind on a particular course.

But Ben knew this was not a good time for Neville to be getting into a brawl, considering what they had planned to do. Neville shrugged off Ben's tug at his sleeve and wheeled back to face Sully, pushing his beer away from the edge of the bar.

"Sully," Darlene warned.

Ben saw it coming. Neville saw it, too. Sully's fist bunched at his side and came up in a short, powerful jab. But Neville was already moving, and the blow glanced off his holster belt as Hallidae's fist curled and came from down low, catching Sully solidly in the gut.

The breath went out of Sully like a pressure valve suddenly sheared off a boiler tank and the miner buckled. Neville stepped in close, and a jarring crash resounded in the close quarters.

Blood gushed freely from between Sully's twisted lips, and that might have ended it for most men. But not for Sully, and not Neville Hallidae. A white-hot rage came into the miner's eyes. He lowered his head and burrowed forward with his fists whirling like the vanes on a stock pump. He caught Neville a solid one on the cheek, and another in the chest. Neville backpedaled with Ben scrambling aside, taking his beer with him.

Sully came on, blind. Neville ducked below

177

his rounding fist, grabbed up a straight-back chair and cracked it to kindling across Sully's side. The big man went down, and sounds of objections came from his companions.

The proprietor stuck his head through the doorway just then. Neville reached around, caught the man by the front of his bib overalls, and hauled him over the bar. With a staggering blow, Jabez Purdy wheeled backward across a table and took it with him in a lumber-snapping crash to the floor.

Neville turned back to Sully with a streak of mean showing itself in his knotted face.

On the floor, Sully groaned and tried to push himself up.

"That's enough," one of the men said, but Neville whacked the toe of his boot hard into Sully's ribs just the same.

Darlene climbed over the bar, catching the hem of her skirts and leaving a strip of gray material draped from the head of a nail. She helped Jabez to his knees and Ben watched him crawl off to a corner, then sit up, dazed.

Two men from Sully's camp came forward.

"Neville," Ben called, grabbing the back of Hallidae's holster belt. Neville swung around like a cock weather vane in a tornado and Ben seized his fist. "Let's get the hell out of here!"

Neville's wild eyes fixed on Ben, dismissed him, and he turned to face the oncomers. Fists and fur flew. Neville could hold his own against these two, but when a third man came along the top of the bar, kicking beer mugs aside, Ben regrettably decided it was either time to get Neville the hell out of there, or lend a hand. Unfortunately, Neville was full-occupied and not of a mind to discuss the matter with him at the moment. Ben slipped behind the bar, snagged this newcomer's pant leg, and heaved him over into the narrow space behind the bar.

The miner crashed on his back, stunned, and Ben dispatched him to a long sleep with a single cuff of his open palm. When Ben stuck his head above the bar, he saw that Neville had handily defeated one of his attackers, and was pouncing all over the other. He caught a glimpse of the one remaining miner slipping out the door. Through the plate glass window, Ben watched him hurry across the street.

"Neville, we got to go," Ben said urgently, vaulting the bar.

"You and your friend aren't going anywhere," Jabez Purdy said, and he held a shotgun.

Ben came up short. Where had he gotten the shotgun? Well, that wasn't important now. What was important was that it was pointed at Neville and himself.

Behind him, Ben heard the sharp smack of

flesh against flesh. The final miner fell straight back like a two-by-twelve plank, raising a small cloud of dust from the floor. Hallidae swung around, taking stock of the situation, and his hand moved dangerously close to the revolver at his side.

"You two keep your hands away from them guns. Don't force me to use this. I don't want to kill nobody."

"Put it up," Ben said reasonably. "We'll leave and no one will get hurt."

Jabez Purdy shook his head with a stubborn look of determination on his face. "You busted up my place, you gonna pay for the damages. We'll just wait for the sheriff."

Ben saw Neville's hand near the worn rubber grips of his Colt. Ben said to Jabez, "Unless you're looking for more blood on your floor, maybe some of your own, maybe some from that pretty wife of yours, you'll put up the shotgun and let us leave here."

"Next blood on this floor is gonna be yours, mister."

Ben had seen Neville move quicker than a stepped-on snake. He could feel the growing tension like a spring clock being wound over-tight. Other than dropping flat to the floor, Ben saw no escaping the shotgun blast.

A shadow cut across the open door and a man stepped in holding a Winchester rifle on them. Back light washed the details from his face, but there was no denying the authority in his stance, and in his words spoken easily but with an edge that warned of their deadly seriousness.

"Fun is over, boys," he said, coming in another step. The man's chin whiskers glowed a rich auburn in the late morning light, and not even the faintest hint of humor revealed itself in the stern line of his mouth. He wore a bowler hat tugged down low over his bushy brows, and a white shirt with blue pinstripes and paper cuffs. The badge pinned to it looked new.

"Easy now. Unbuckle them belts and don't try anything foolish. Between Jabez and me, you boys are definitely through for the day."

Ben and Neville dropped their gun belts.

"Kick 'em aside. Jabez, collect 'em, please," the sheriff said once the weapons were out of reach.

Jabez handed Darlene the shotgun and snatched away the holsters as if they'd been near the mouth of a sleeping grizzly bear, backing quickly to his wife's side.

The sheriff eased up then. "You two got names? Don't recollect seeing the likes of you here in Alpine before."

Ben glanced at Neville. The outlaw leader

had no intention of giving the sheriff that information.

"Well," the sheriff said, seeing that neither one of them intended to talk, "you'll have plenty of time to remember them while you cool your heels in jail."

Darlene said, "I heard them call each other Ben and Neville."

"Ben and Neville?" The sheriff regarded them, then seemed suddenly to make a connection. "You two wouldn't be the Ben and Neville what held up the bank over Buena Vista way last week? Got word of it only yesterday." The sheriff glanced at Jabez and a twitch of humor broke the stern line of his mouth. "I think you might of caught yourself a couple of real lunkers here, Jabez."

The proprietor looked startled at first. Then he, too, was grinning. "There a reward for 'em, sheriff?"

"Seems to me I did read that they had a price on their heads. If these two are from that gang, Jabez, you and the missus will come into a sizable piece of change."

Ben glanced at Neville. Outwardly, Hallidae looked unconcerned, but inside, Ben knew the man was about to burst wide open despite the guns turned on him.

Ben's thoughts came to a halt then. The guns held on them really only amounted to one gun! The woman would only hit the ceiling with her shotgun if she pulled the trigger now. Ben's thoughts raced ahead, in a glance he assessed the situation. He spied the mug of beer on the bar at his elbow and, in an instant, came to a decision.

Nineteen

The sheriff was grinning now. He said to Jabez, "It was a federal marshal up from the Territories who identified them. Seems he's been tagging after these two and some others for more than a month. They're called the Hallidae Gang, and the leader is a fellow named Neville." The lawman regarded Neville with some curiosity. "That wouldn't happen to be you now, would it, mister?"

Neville considered the sheriff narrowly, partly because his eye was beginning to swell shut, and did not answer.

As the sheriff was full-occupied with Neville, Ben took the opportunity to ease his elbow back upon the bar. Jabez and Darlene had found Neville the more interesting of the two of them, too. Neither of them noticed Ben's hand slide behind and cup the beer mug.

Only half-aware that his thoughts were traveling backward, Ben became a boy once more, with Joe Ratkin and Jimmy Singer at the palisades overlooking the Missouri River. Jimmy was lobbing a ponderous rock out over the edge. It didn't go very far before it turned a wide arch in the air and began its long descent toward the brown waters that eddied around the root of those lofty cliffs a hundred feet below. Ben eyed the falling target, hitched back his arm, and took aim with one of the smooth river rocks he'd carried up in his pockets. . . .

The beer mug sailed out across the long room, and before anyone knew what was happening, it smacked the lawman square in the face like the hind hooves of a startled mule.

His rifle fired, sending the bullet screaming past Ben to shatter bottles behind the bar. Ben dove for the carbine and wrenched it free of the sheriff's grip. He took two steps and easily snatched the shotgun from the proprietor's startled and wide-eyed wife, and then with both arms hefting firearms, Ben took his first quick breath and glanced swiftly around the room.

It all had happened so suddenly that only when it was over did Neville begin to appreciate the new hand dealt around.

The sheriff slumped against the wall to the floor. Blood made a sudden bright appearance through the hand covering his face, and ran down his wrist, over his chin. His eyes glazed over and moisture flowed freely from them. A fellow at the door who had come in with the sheriff bent to his aide.

"Nobody move," Ben ordered, sweeping

the narrow room with the muzzle of the shotgun. With his other hand, he pointed the Winchester at Jabez. "Put those here."

Jabez hooked the holster belts over the end of the rifle barrel. Ben tipped it up and let them slide onto his arm. "Now, back over there, against the wall."

The proprietor and his wife moved aside, showing no inclination to debate the order.

Neville said, "Shoot 'em, Ben. Don't wait to think about it."

Ben found himself wavering. To let these people live would be dangerous, but would it be more dangerous than killing them? Tom had said that when no blood was spilled, the law wasn't nearly so anxious to follow. Ben tended to agree. Neville urged differently now, but for some odd reason, Ben could hear Andy's voice pulling him the other way.

"Let's get the hell out of here, Neville."

"We can't leave them alive knowing what they do."

The faces around Ben had frozen in various degrees of interest and terror, bleached like so much deadwood left for years in the sun.

"We're leaving, Neville." The determination in Ben's voice made it clear the subject was not open to debate.

Neville came forward. Ben shifted the shotgun, bringing him up short. His words came low and firm. "I said, we are leaving."

The outlaw leader scorched Ben with a look that teetered on the edge of rage. Ben held fast while the people standing around waited to see who would win out, who would decide their fate.

"They know who we are, Ben," Neville said through his growing anger.

But that didn't so much concern Ben as the amount of time they were wasting there. He glanced at the doorway expecting at any moment to see armed men bursting their way through. "Stay if you want, Neville. I'm leaving, and I'm taking them with me."

Ben moved toward the doorway with the holster belts slung over his shoulder, wheeling both the rifle and shotgun wide to cover the men standing there. They gave way before him like the opening of a door. The next instant, Ben was swinging up onto his horse and turning it away.

Of a sudden, Neville was there beside him and mounted too. Somehow — later, Ben could not remember the details of it clearly — they kicked their animals into a full gallop and pounded down that crowded street and out of town as if not another soul was around to bar their way.

"If I don't get some water, we won't have

fresh bread tonight." Wilson made it sound like a mild threat, as he built up a large fire to burn down into a thick bed of coals. His look glanced off Andoreana, then moved over to where Tom was reclining. "Think you could go fetch me some, Tom?"

"It's too early to be starting bread," Tom answered. He'd found just enough tobacco in a pocket of his rucksack to make up one more cigarette, and he was smoking it now as if there were no more Bull Durham left in the entire world.

Andoreana could see his enjoyment, and his irritation at Turner's attempt to tear him away from it, and she wondered why Turner pressed on so. Even at her age, she knew well enough when someone wanted to be left alone. But Wilson seemed not to care.

She looked back at Susie Meyers and fussed with the doll, but with little enthusiasm for play. That part of her had died in the fire with her mother and brother. Yet there was a certain comfort in the cloth and cotton figure, even if there was no warmth. She spoke softly to Susie Meyers and desperately searched for some of the old happy feelings to return . . . but they did not.

Tom's yelp startled her and she glanced over in time to see the stub of his cigarette arch through the air and land near the fire pit. He sucked his forefinger but, despite the sting of the cigarette, an easy, satisfied grin filled his wide face. "Ummm-um, that was good," he said with deep feeling, leaning back against his saddle, eyes closed and turned up to the bright blue bowl overhead.

Turner was watching her again with that peculiar glint in his eye that made her uneasy in a way she did not understand. Her attention shifted to the black man.

"If you are all done and satisfied now, maybe you'll go fetch me some water."

Tom Deveraux opened his eyes and studied the little man hunched over the fire pit with exasperation showing all over his face. "You sure can be tiresome when you don't get your own way, Wilson."

"Seems as though I'm the only one working around here," he complained, casting an accusing glance at Mcintyre as well.

Scott set the saddlebag and stitching awl down and said, "Since when did you become our mother hen?"

Wilson's glare bore down on him and cut short his complaint. Mcintyre averted his eyes. Andoreana saw the thin line of victory come to Turner's lips. He looked back at Tom. "Well, how about it?"

"Like I said, you can be darn pesky." Tom tightened up the laces of his boots. He stood and picked the canvas water bucket off a broken tree limb.

"I'll be back."

"Take your time," Turner said easily, "I still have to let the coals burn down."

Tom turned back and regarded Wilson with open exasperation, then he tramped off over the ridge and down the long slope to the stream below.

Wilson's grin moved to Andoreana. Throwing a final look in the direction Tom had gone, he got up and stood over her. "You're too old to play with dolls, Andy."

"I am not."

He hunkered down. "Sure you are. A gal your age ought to be learning what women are all about."

"Sir?"

"Don't go simple on me. You know what I'm talking about." His grin, Andoreana thought, had turned most unpleasant, and she felt something was terribly wrong here, but had only a vague notion of what that might be.

"I think I'll go along with Mr. Deveraux," she said, and tried to stand, but Turner pushed her roughly back.

"You hurt me," Andoreana said.

The grin widened. "That's not my intention at all," he said, rolling the flimsy material of

190

her nightgown between his thumb and finger.

"Turner?" Mcintyre was standing, looking concerned. "What you up to, Turner?"

Wilson wheeled around angrily. "Why don't you go find something to do, Fish Brain? Something that will keep you out of my hair for about the next fifteen minutes."

Andoreana watched the pain come to Mcintyre's face. It was a tortured look, and she wanted desperately for him to stay in camp now.

"Turner," he said, and it sounded almost like a plea. "Don't go and do that."

Wilson sprang forward. The big bowie knife flashed in the sunlight. Mcintyre cowered. "I said get out of here, Fish Brain."

Mcintyre looked at Andoreana with sadness in his eyes, then at the big knife and Wilson's contorted face. His cheek quivered as he backed down and took up his hat. He tugged it on and, without another look, dropped his head and walked off into the trees.

Wilson rotated slowly on his heels and his thoughts made themselves plain upon his face. "Now," he said, sheathing the knife, "let old Turner show you what it means to be a grown-up girl." And he advanced on her.

Andoreana stood, knowing something terrible was about to happen. Her bare toes dug nervously into the cool earth. Her arms

191

squeezed Susie Meyers with a fear that would have suffocated flesh and blood.

"First thing we do is take off that old night-gown," he said, standing over her, tall and terrible.

"No!"

His hand snapped out. Andoreana turned away from him, hearing the rent of tearing cloth. The cool mountain air touched her naked shoulders, but even so, the heat of her fear raced through her body, and she was only vaguely aware of it as she ran across the camp, clutching the doll and the remains of her nightgown to herself.

Turner Wilson laughed softly as he came after her, but there was no humor on his face, only an ugly snarl. Andoreana wanted to cry out for her papa, but fear choked her. All she was aware of was the man approaching, and then she was aware of cold rock pressing against her back, and the ground falling steeply away a few feet to her right where the valley was.

"Well, seems you backed yourself into a corner, Andy."

She wanted to plead with him, but then she remembered Mcintyre and resolved that she would never plead. She would fight, and she would lose — but she would fight just the same. When Wilson bent near to her, Andoreana lashed out with a fury, her nails clawing blindly.

Somewhere in the struggle Susie Meyers slipped from her grasp. Her nails drew blood and Turner cried out, throwing his hands to his face. She ducked under his arms and snatched a burning stick from the fire.

"You little bitch," Turner snarled, dragging a hand across his face and staring at the blood upon it. In blind rage he picked up the doll and took his knife to it, slashing it and ripping out the cotton stuffing. He tossed it far over the edge of the valley, where it fell out of sight and out of Andoreana's life.

Turner wheeled back to face Andoreana. The knife in his hand moved like a deadly snake ready to strike. "All right," he said with a calm that precedes a storm. "You want it rough, I'll give it to you rough."

Andoreana braced herself with the stick held tightly in her small hands. Its flame had died to a glowing red tip.

"You stay away from me!" she cried. "You're a bad man. You rob banks and hurt people!"

"Who told you that?"

At once Andoreana realized her mistake.

"It was Ben, wasn't it?"

Andoreana knew she should deny it, but that would be a lie. And she would not allow this

193

evil man to make her tell a lie.

But her silence was all the admission Turner needed. "I'll see to him later," he said, and then he lunged at her.

Twenty

From Andoreana's frightened point of view, it was as if Turner Wilson had had a rope tied around his shoulders and someone big and strong had come up behind him and given it a mighty tug.

Andoreana had not seen who that *someone* might have been, for her eyes had been rigidly fixed upon Turner, upon the knife that threw back the morning sunlight, and upon his wicked leer. She shifted her weight nervously and waved the miserable little stick above her head trying to look menacing, somehow knowing that neither she nor it were any match for the crazed man coming at her.

Thus occupied, Andoreana Dean did not see Tom Deveraux come up behind Wilson. She did not suspect that anyone was near to help her until the smaller man lurched suddenly backward.

Turner sprawled on the ground in a heap, and Tom stood over him. "I knew you was up to no good." He gathered Wilson up by his shirt front in one hand and curled the other into a fist and drove it deep into Wilson's gut.

The knife glinted as it cartwheeled into the

air. Wilson hit the ground hard again —
spread-eagled, not moving at first, then slowly
he rolled to his side, clambered to hands and
knees and glared up at the big Negro standing
before him.

"Son-of-a-bitch nigger," Wilson hissed
through the ragged yellow line of his clenched
teeth.

Tom was ready and sidestepped easily as
Wilson sprang. He clipped Turner solidly on
the chin as he passed, and the smaller man
went down again for a third time. He came
up confused, then he found Deveraux, who
by this time had moved around behind him.

Andoreana scrambled out of their way,
pressing her spine up against a tree, watching
the two men circle, seeking an advantage over
each other. Tom was the stronger, but Wilson
grabbed for the revolver at his side.

In a quick move for a man his size, Tom
struck out with the toe of his boot and kicked
the gun from Turner's hand.

Lunging, Wilson grappled Tom's boot as
it swung by. He wrenched his leg around and
Deveraux pitched over backward. Stunned, he
lay there long enough for Wilson to stagger
to his feet.

Wilson cast frantically around and spied the
bowie lying a dozen feet off. He leaped into
a rolling dive, grabbing the knife up. But by

that time Tom was back on his feet and around they went, Deveraux with his arms wide, dodging back whenever the smaller man plunged the broad knife at him. Wilson tried again and again for an opening. Each attack missed, yet each drove Deveraux farther back toward the rocks that rose up at the valley's edge.

Andoreana's heart almost leaped from her chest when Tom finally came up against the boulders and realized all at once that he had been boxed in. Through the haze of his frenzy, Wilson, too, realized the advantage he had finally won. He ceased his advance to size up the situation.

Andoreana's hope melted. She knew of no way to help Tom against that large, curved blade.

The savage contortions on Wilson's face relaxed into a confident grin. "Looks like you backed yourself into a corner there, Cotton." His voice quavered, still out of control. "It's the last corner you're gonna see this side of Glory."

The black man's wide eyes swayed with the bowie knife, like the hypnotized snake in a basket Andoreana had once seen in a book about India.

Suddenly Wilson flipped the knife over and caught it by the tip in a practiced manner that

Andoreana had seen him rehearse time and time again.

"Too much of a coward to use your fists?" Tom said. Andoreana could see him casting about for some avenue of escape.

Wilson only laughed.

"I'd be a fool to give you back the advantage, nigger!" he said, and with that his arm cocked back. . . .

Although patience usually panned out for him in the end, Walt Devon was having a difficult time not allowing his impatience to spur him now from his carefully thought-out course and drive him heedlessly up over the Continental Divide, where he suspected Neville Hallidae already was — or would be shortly.

He was determined to keep to his planned course of riding an ever-widening circle, knowing full well that one of these times he would have to cross Neville Hallidae's trail, and then he'd have his man.

Devon heard Franklin Dean's horse scramble from behind. The anxious father drew up beside him and said, "If we split up, we could cover more ground, Marshal."

Devon halted and the two deputies who had been ranging off to either side reined in as well, as if they had only been waiting for an excuse to stretch and come out of their saddles. Stanley Hedstrom swung down and did a couple of deep kneebends. Landy arched back, pressing his fingertips into his spine. The unrelenting drive was taking a toll on their backs and the less popular parts of their anatomy, but Devon could live with it, and so could these young deputies.

"You do what you think necessary, Dean. But you do it alone. I don't intend to split my deputies among us."

"It makes sense, don't it?"

Devon understood the father's torment but it was not his nature to allow sympathy to interfere with his work. Perhaps that was what had come between him and Ferro all those years ago, Devon thought ruefully. If he had been more the understanding father and less the dogged lawman, maybe —

Devon cut short that line of thinking. It was old ground, and barren, and he put away for the moment any speculation about his son, and how he might have raised the boy differently.

The only thing that mattered now was finding Neville Hallidae and, if Dean's daughter was among them, getting her back if he could. He said, "I need every pair of eyes with me, Dean. I have invested a lot of time tracking these men and I don't intend for it to go sour by dividing my men and having them off beating the bushes on their own."

Devon rocked back in his saddle, regarding the strained face staring back at him, and he found a bit of compassion rearing its head in his determined heart. He said, "I'm going to find these men, and if your daughter is with them, you'll have her back."

"If?"

"That's still the question, isn't it?"

"And if she isn't?"

He didn't have a good answer to that question. "Then I reckon your search starts all over again, Dean," he said flatly, turning his animal and moving away up the rocky slope where not too many hundred feet overhead the trees ended. Above that the entire buttress of the Continental Divide raised its mighty gray granite walls to the blue sky. A place of shrubs, and sere grass, and year-round snow. A cold, unfriendly realm that Walt Devon was not anxious to invade. Yet somehow before all this was over, he knew he would have to.

Ben Masters came upon them and sized up the situation in a glance. He heard Wilson's final words, saw the smaller man's arm cocking back for the throw. Ben pulled his revolver and fired a shot into the air.

Wilson spun around and Andy nearly bit

off a fingertip at the report of his revolver. Wilson glared at Ben, and Tom Deveraux breathed a word of thanks.

"Put the knife up."

Wilson quivered; he was a steel trap set and ready to spring, and it could go either way. Ben leveled his revolver and drew back the hammer. "I'm not going to tell you again. Drop that knife or I'll drop you, Wilson."

In the moment that passed, Ben was aware of the blood pounding in his ears. Every small sound seemed louder than he was accustomed to. Wilson quavered, weighing, it seemed to Ben, the yeas and nays of what to do next. With a moan of frustration, Wilson wheeled away and let the knife fly into the trunk of a blue spruce. He cussed and kicked dirt into the coals of his fire, then picked his gun and hat off the ground and stomped angrily away.

Ben could see that Tom was scared, although he tried not to show it. "You sure enough picked a fine time to come back, Ben." Then Deveraux saw Neville Hallidae's raw and purple face, and the look of subdued rage upon his unsmiling face.

"What happened to you, Neville?"

Hallidae swung off his horse and, in a stilted gait, walked over to the fire, picked the coffeepot out of the coals, and poured himself a cup from what remained.

Tom glanced at Ben.

Ben grimaced. "Tell me what happened here."

Tom did, briefly, and when he'd finished, Ben went to Andy, still flush against the tree, eyes wide and fixed. She seemed to hesitate as he hunkered down beside her, and then as if at the opening of a gate, she burst into tears and flung her arms tightly around his neck.

"It's all right now." Ben held her. A big, half-grown child filled his arms. When she had finished crying, he carried her over to his horse, set her down, and lifted the bulging flour sack off the saddle.

"I brought you something, Andy."

"What?" A little enthusiasm brightened her eyes. Mcintyre came back into camp just then. Ben felt Andy stiffen. Scott glanced at them as he scuffed past, then he turned his eyes down to the ground and went off to his bedroll and sat without a word.

It seemed to Ben no one was saying much, and the electricity in the air was like that before a thunderstorm. He figured it would pass. Yet a lingering bit of doubt tugged at him on this point as he opened the sack and brought out the supplies and gifts he had purchased in Alpine.

Twenty-one

"That kid ain't caused nothing but trouble from the minute we took her in," Wilson grumbled. But no one was listening to him, least of all Neville Hallidae.

Hallidae was in a pensive state, brooding into his steaming cup of coffee, his fourth since coming back into camp. Ben knew that when the man was like this, deep into serious thought, it was something to be noted. Whenever Neville got into one of his meditative moods, things began to change.

"I wasn't gonna hurt the kid," Wilson went on, whining. "Wasn't gonna hurt Cotton none, neither, except he went and made me mad."

The afternoon had turned gray, and clouds churned angrily against the bare-rock peaks above them. It was not unusual for the weather to get fearsome and unpredictable at higher elevations, and Ben figured this might be a good time to break out the dog tents. At least they would each have a blanket tonight.

Andy protested when she saw the shoes and the britches Ben had brought her. She told him she did not wear pants. She wore dresses as a proper girl ought to. But when Ben pointed out that it was either the new pants or her old ripped nightgown, Andy shut her mouth and took the clothes around the backside of a rock.

Everything fit in a passable manner. She used a steel mirror Ben kept in his toilette kit to check it all over properly, frowning, but saying nothing further about the clothes. Ben helped her roll the pant legs up to the right height and then they spent some time poking around the slope beyond the camp. But they could not find any trace of Susie Meyers, except for a few tufts of cotton stuffing.

"I say it's time we dump her." Turner was carrying on to no one's particular interest. "We used to be one big happy family before —"

Tom's laugh was a deep, sarcastic rumble like the thunder they had been hearing on and off for the last hour. He said, "You're dreamin' Turner. We ain't never been but two steps from jumping all over each other."

"Maybe so," Wilson came back. "But at least we was loyal, one to the other. At least, we didn't go telling our business to outsiders." He looked pointedly at Ben. Neville's eyes came up at this, turning toward Ben, too. Far off in the distance, thunder rolled like kettle drums from far back in the mountains and boomed through the valley.

Ben rose and dug through the pile of supplies and came back with the dog tents, each one rolled up with its sticks. He made himself busy setting them up. Neville had moved over to the fire, poured himself another cup of coffee, and was consulting in low tones and guarded glances with Turner Wilson.

The wind picked up by midday, gusting off the peaks in chill blasts. The five of them had gathered close around the pit of coals cooking bacon and a steak from the hind quarter of an elk Mcintyre had shot earlier. Neville Hallidae eyed each man as though weighing a major decision, then with a smoking brand he picked out of the fire, he drew a wavy line in the dirt.

"This here is the Continental Divide," he said, speaking softly. Hallidae lifted his chin at the wall of bare granite that grew to the west of them and winced where the raw skin pulled tight. His left eye had swollen nearly closed. "Right up there a couple thousand feet, that is if you measure your distances straight up instead of flat out."

Tom made a low depreciating laugh in his throat. "Only birds and angels measure it that way."

Neville went on as if he had not heard. "We can cross off the job at Alpine." He made an X in the ground beside the squiggle line of the Divide. "They know who we are and they'll surely be waiting for us." He lowered his view toward Ben a moment, then went on quickly. "And we can't wait around this part of Colorado very long, either. That marshal from down in the Territories has found his way up here somehow, and knowing him, it won't be long before he figures out where we are. Besides, winter will be closing in on us in another month and I want to be long gone before then."

"We still going north to Idaho?" Turner asked with the eagerness of a boy taking off on a holiday.

"Idaho is where we are heading. We aren't wanted for anything there, and if we do it right, we'll be far enough away that Devon won't never find us."

"I didn't know U.S. Marshals had any say-so in the states, Neville," Mcintyre said.

"Whether they do or don't, it don't make no difference to a man like Devon. He goes where he pleases, does what he wants."

"Still, even in Idaho, anything we do might tip off a man like that," Tom advised.

Neville nodded his head rather gently, Ben thought. Ben glanced over his shoulder at Andy, who watched them from the open end of the dog tent with her new blanket pulled up tight over her shoulders, sucking on a lemon sugar stick. Ben had told her to stay put and had given her the brown paper bag of candy and a cup of tea to warm her while she waited.

Ben looked back at the fire aware that a change had come over Neville, still not able to read what the man was thinking. Neville wasn't talking about it.

Neville continued in a low voice, "That's why we aren't gonna do anything to tip him off. We have made us up a goodly size poke as it is. I figure one more quick job to fatten it enough to last out a couple of seasons and then we hightail it west and north, putting on our best manners. Even Devon isn't gonna keep dogging a cold trace. And I mean, we'll make it dead cold as a Confederate graveyard."

That riveted Ben's attention. It was an odd expression; one he'd never heard Neville use before. He caught a glancing look from the outlaw leader. Ben had never had any reason to inquire of Hallidae's politics on the war, but Neville was from Ohio and that just about said it all. Ben, on the other hand, being from Missouri, knew his leanings were less clear.

But maybe he was wearing his feelings too close to the surface. He tried to dismiss the uneasiness that had come over him and returned his stare to the wind-brightening coals beneath the roast of elk.

"What do you have in mind, Neville?" Turner Wilson asked.

Neville said, "We pull off another job here in Colorado." He maintained his voice low enough that it did not travel beyond the five of them. "Then just as quick as we can, we hop on over to Utah. Spend some time moving around, maybe feign a southernly direction, and once the snows come, we hurry on up north. If we can make Devon think we're gonna winter down in Arizona, which any practical man might choose to do, we can run him onto a cold trail. He'll never find our trace once it's two, three months old."

Neville's lips settled into a smile. "Once in Idaho, we can light easy a while. Maybe once the heat is off, head west to Oregon, or even California. I'm not wanted for anything anywhere that far west. Any of you?"

"I am," Mcintyre said softly.

"How long back?"

Mcintyre shrugged his meaty shoulders. "Five, six years ago. I'm not worried. That was south, Los Angeles Pueblo. California is a long state, lots of places to get lost in. I hear San Francisco is nice."

Neville looked at Turner. "You?"

Wilson shook his head.

"How 'bout you, Ben?"

"Never been to California before. Don't reckon I'm wanted for anything there yet."

Neville regarded Tom, started to ask him, then stopped and shook his head. "No, I don't suppose you've ever been to California, either."

Tom allowed that he hadn't. Arizona was as far west as he had ever gotten, and he appreciated Arizona's warm winters and did not look with much eagerness to a cold-sounding place like Idaho.

"Except for Mcintyre, we are all clean in California. Well, it don't matter. Like you said, it's a big state."

"And no Marshal Devon in it," Mcintyre added with a short laugh.

Hallidae poked his stick into the ground on the other side of the squiggle line. "Then listen now. Here is what we are gonna do. Tomorrow we will make our way up over the Divide. It will be hard traveling and long, but not far beyond, and a goodly distance lower, is a boom place that has become a center of money transfers for the mining district since the Denver & South Park Road came through."

"How do you know all this?" Ben asked him.

"There was talk in Buena Vista that the county seat might even be moved there. I bent an ear and learned that there are over twenty-five hundred folks living there and the population is growing every month. They even got two banks so we have a choice. A map of the entire district was in the assay office. All I had to do was study it.

"If we move quickly, we can make us a big haul and be out of the area before they know what hit them. Maybe we'll even buy passage on the Denver & Rio Grande Western Road at Gunnison and ride it clear to the other side of the state. That would put distance between us and Devon."

Hallidae's eyes gleamed despite his bruised and battered face. Turner Wilson was grinning too, and even Mcintyre had come out of his despondency enough to show a wide row of teeth. As usual, Tom was complacent. No matter what plans they made, he always ended up staying behind with the horses.

But Ben found his uneasiness growing. He glanced back at Andy with a gnawing bit of concern. Neville had made no mention of dropping the child off. How far did he intend to take her?

"What's the name of this boom place, Neville?" Turner asked.

Hallidae grinned and reached for the coffeepot. "It's called Pitkin. The future economic center of the Tincup mining district, and our personal plum."

Hallidae raised his cup of coffee. "Here's to Pitkin. Our last job."

Turner was about the only one who seemed overly thrilled with Neville's plans as he spread a canvas sheet around his shoulders and hunched over the fire to protect it from the coming rain.

Mcintyre crawled off to his squat little tent and in a while the noise of a harmonica came through its canvas walls. Tom hauled his rucksack into his own, extracting a pouch of Bull Durham as he lay on his stomach upon his bedroll.

The cold drops began thumping with regularity, exploding like small artillery shells on the dry ground. Each man made for his own tent — except Turner, who was staying behind to protect the fire.

Ben remained uneasy. He stooped into his tent, where Andy was waiting quietly for him, and the storm washed over them as though heavenly floodgates had burst open. Through the gray slanting wind-driven sheets, he almost lost sight of Turner all together where he hunched above the fire under his canvas sheet.

For the next hour lightning battled the mountainside like flint against steel, and thunder shook the ground. And Ben's feeling of uneasiness deepened as he thought about Pitkin, and what might lay ahead for Andy afterward.

Twenty-two

"There goes their trail, Marshal," Landy said with easy resignation. He had long ago lost hope of ever catching up with the Hallidae Gang.

They had come upon a hollow gouged out of the mountainside as if by an enormous ice cream scoop, and had ridden under its cover only moments before the storm rumbled over them.

Devon leaned heavily against the outer edge, watching the land beyond turn to lead. Rain drummed off the upper rim of their alcove and seemed to hang suspended, like a beaded curtain strung up in front of the opening, digging a muddy trench across the entrance at the tip of Devon's boot. He was tired, and he pretended not to hear Landy's remark. He knew that no one but himself and Franklin Dean shared a particular zeal for running down Neville Hallidae. It was just a job to them.

He'd have to reconsider the idea of crossing Hallidae's trail now with this rain scouring the land. The thought irked him, yet his face remained immovable, like the crumbling granite arch around him.

Lightning scattered their shadows against the back of the shallow cave. The horses side-stepped nervously into each other. Hedstrom and Dean tightened their grip upon the reins and spoke in soothing tones.

"What are your plans now, Marshal?" Landy said, louder this time, so Devon couldn't feign deafness. Devon turned. A heavy, weary-of-body turn, but his dark eyes shone with restless fire. The lightning outside flashed in them.

"My plans don't change with the weather, deputy."

Landy's easy smile hardened, and he seemed to be waging an internal battle to keep his eyes fixed upon the marshal's. Devon had no desire to intimidate his deputies, though often his size and dogged determination did just that. He went back to watching the storm melt away Neville Hallidae's trace.

"You just don't ever quit, do you?"

"Quit?" Devon's eyes remained fixed upon the leaden curtain drawn across the landscape. "A man quits when he's dead, deputy. Of course, some men quit before then, and I guess afterward they aren't worth much more than if they were already in the grave. Fact is, when a man stops pushing, he's inviting the grim reaper to come for him."

Devon glanced at Landy. "I, on the other

hand, prefer to keep that old timer and his reaping scythe at bay as long as the Good Lord gives me breath and the strength to do so. How old are you?"

The question caught Landy off-guard. "Twenty-two," he answered warily.

Devon gave a short laugh and turned back to the storm. "I got more than thirty years on you, son. Don't tell me a young fellow like you can't keep up with an old man like me."

"I can keep up with you just fine, Marshal," Landy shot back with an angry resolve in his voice.

Devon felt the need for a grin just then, but he kept it bottled up behind the stern mask that watched and waited for the storm to pass.

"They come on like this, and then just as suddenly" — he snapped a finger in the air as if to illustrate — "it's all over. Sun comes out and dries everything up — well, almost everything." He grinned. "That street out front turns to gumbo and it might take days for it to dry."

He smiled disarmingly at her, but all that Kathleen Hamil could see was the growing puddle of muddy water on the floor around his boots, and Kelvin McKormick's impatient glance settling sternly upon her from his cubical at the back of the store.

"That's very interesting, Mr. Geckhorn," she said, distracted. *Now, where was it that McKormick kept the bucket and mop?*

"Oh, you can call me Harlan. I don't mind."

"What?"

"Harlan . . . my name?"

"Yes, of course. Ah — was there something you wanted, Sheriff?"

"No, no. I'm just making my rounds, that's all."

"In the rain?" She glanced incredulously at the water streaming down the windowpane up front.

Harlan Geckhorn laughed. "I can't let something like a little rain keep me from my business, now can I?"

McKormick cleared his throat. His unexpected appearance at Geckhorn's side startled the sheriff. "Ye have been making quite a few rounds this day, I would say." McKormick regarded the sheriff with a suspicious scowl.

Geckhorn's neck reddened. The glow of it crawled up to his cheeks. "Have I?" His laugh went high, and a little uncertain. "Well, I got a lot to watch over, don't I? Guess I better be getting on with it now," he said as if suddenly perceiving the scope of the task ahead of him. He tipped his hat, adding a trickle to the puddle on the floor, and hurried back out into the rain.

216

Kathleen let go of an impatient breath. "He certainly is an industrious man, isn't he?"

"Hummm," McKormick replied, studying her over the rim of his spectacles. "The mop is in back," he said, and returned to his cubicle.

The sun engaged the angry, black clouds and subdued them after a lengthy battle, dissolving them across a widening blue sky into fleeing gray wisps. In the aftermath, the air was fresh and washed, and somewhere among the dripping forest a Steller's jay sang out with a joyful *wheck — wek — wek — wek — wek,* announcing that the storm had passed and that everyone could get back to their business.

Andy was holding the bar of White Rose Glycerine Soap to her nose when Ben suddenly slapped the canvas all over, sending a spray of water like a dog after a swim.

"Looks like the storm has passed, Andy."

She glanced up at him sharply.

He grinned. "One would think you would get used to it by this time."

"My name is Andoreana," she advised curtly.

Ben laughed and folded himself out of the low dog tent. Turner Wilson uncovered his head cautiously. The fire had fared far better than he through the ordeal. Turner lifted off the canvas sheet, eyes smoke-reddened, smelling of pine resin and smoke — an improvement, Ben thought. The coals beneath the elk steak brightened fiercely in the clean breeze.

"You saved the fire and dinner," Ben said gregariously, feeling suddenly large and vigorous in the aftermath. He poured himself a cup of coffee.

Turner shook the canvas at him and laughed when Ben flinched away. Turner threw the wet sheet across a nearby boulder to dry as the others emerged to add their footprints to the muddied campsite.

Andy tiptoed upon the mud to Tom's tent.

"Hello, there, chil'," Tom said, stretching.

"Mr. Deveraux? Will you read some more about Huckleberry Finn to me?"

Tom glanced at the clearing sky, judging the amount of daylight left. "I suppose I could do that. Too late to pack up and pull out of here, too early to go to bed." Grinning, he reached around into the rucksack and came back holding the leather-bound book. "You just sit you'self down there, chil', and you and me will see what happens to Huck and old Jim on the river."

Tom eased himself onto his ground sheet next to Andy, anchoring the heels of his big boots in the mud outside the tent, and started to read aloud.

Turner went on fixing dinner and getting the evening pot of beans to boiling. The others, more or less occupied, seemed to find that their chores drew them near to Tom's tent. And even Neville — although Ben suspected he'd deny it if confronted — seemed more than mildly interested in Huck's affairs, even though Ben seemed to recall that Neville had once called it "nigger trash."

When dinner was ready, Andy passed the new bar of soap around to all, but none of the men seemed interested in it. Her call to say grace was met with more resistance, and a loud round of grumbling from Turner.

Neville said flatly, "None of that anymore."

"Let the kid say it if she wants to," Tom Deveraux came back in her behalf.

Ben Masters said to her, "You go ahead if you want, Andy, and say it."

She did.

Turner hissed.

Mcintyre was standing some distance away watching the orange glow of a finished day languish against the western peaks. He'd been in a cheerless mood since the morning incident, and now as Andy began the prayer, he turned deliberately from them and seemed to say in the defiant arch of his back that he wanted nothing to do with it either.

Ben sensed that some very definite lines had been drawn. Their normal dinner bantering had degenerated into questions briefly stated, and answered more often than not in a single grunt. Through it all, Andy seemed oblivious to the growing turmoil, still lost in the tragedy of her own life but showing the amazing resiliency of youth. She'd make out all right, Ben knew — and be better off the sooner he could get her away from the trouble brewing here between the five of them.

Tom nearly finished up Huck's tale that night and promised Andy he'd read the final chapters to her at their next camp.

When night came, the sky was perfectly innocent of the storm that had swept through earlier, spread out with enough stars to give a cool, silvery glow to the ground and the bare peaks above them. They each found their way to their dog tents and let the fire burn itself out.

Ben folded over an end of his ground sheet for Andy and stepped out into the shadow for a moment. When he returned, the girl was already asleep. In place of the doll, she clutched the bunched-up remains of her nightgown.

He watched her, frowning, and glanced at Turner Wilson's tent.

The camp was quiet when Ben crawled between his blankets and bunched his coat up under his head. He didn't believe Wilson would try further for the girl, but just the same he laid out his Colt where its cool, hard grip fell conveniently to hand at his head. Then he worked his hips into the shallow depression beneath his bedroll. The day had been particularly wearisome for Ben, and it had come on the heels of a night of little sleep. Almost immediately upon closing his eyes, he felt the morning urging him awake again.

Twenty-three

Ben rolled out of his blankets, working the kinks from his back as he bent over the fire pit, blowing across the coals in search of any latent life there. He coaxed an ember into a flame, nursed it with kindling, then fed it a couple good-sized logs. He carried the water bucket down to the stream and had a proper fire blazing and a pot of coffee boiling by the time Neville made an appearance.

The outlaw leader glanced up at the sky with approval in his still-swollen face and said, "Don't have time to dally today, Ben." He indicated the gray peaks ahead. "I want to be over the Divide by noon. Yesterday's storm washed away any tracks we left behind. It'll slow up that old marshal some. The more distance we put between him and us, the easier I'll feel. Coffee done?"

"Almost," Ben said, feeling the unspoken tension in the other man.

Neville went over and nudged the feet under the blankets of the others. "No sleeping in this morning." He ignored their groans and complaints as he came back and bent for the perking pot to pour himself a cup of coffee.

"We will be in Pitkin tonight, you and me, Ben, checking out the bank. Tomorrow I want to take it early and be twenty miles or more away by night."

They broke camp at once. Tom and Scott secured the *aparejo* onto the mule and loaded everything onto it, working back and forth with the rope to tie it down tight in a practiced diamond hitch.

Each gnawing only a strip of hard jerky apiece for breakfast, they climbed upon the backs of their horses. Ben gave Andy a hand up and she settled herself on Ben's bedroll behind his saddle. "All ready for traveling in your new outfit?"

"I'm ready," she said. "I guess I'm not going to need this any longer, am I, Uncle Ben?"

He eyed the dirty scrap of cloth that had once been a nightgown and remembered how she had taken comfort in her sleep with it as she had her doll. "You can keep it if you want to."

"No," she said after some thought. "It makes me sad."

"I understand, Andy."

She dropped the nightgown to the ground and wrapped her arms around his waist, and their horses trampled the tattered cloth into the drying mud as they pulled out and began the formidable climb to the Divide.

Tall spruce gave way to gnarled, arthritic trees and shrubs, beaten close to the ground by the eternal chill winds of this high, naked land. Tree line. Sere grass and lichen-covered boulders. Their horses pushed on, heads bent against icy blasts off the snow-capped pinnacles that stood immovable against the impossibly blue sky, frowning down upon the travelers. They followed an old trail, first scraped into the rocky ground by migrating elk, and then later widened and straightened by the feet of generations of Ute Indians. The trail skirted the highest of the peaks and angled steadily upward toward an exposed saddle of gray rock that bowed between two fourteen-thousand footers.

Ben pulled on his frock coat and helped Andy tuck a blanket around her shoulders. He didn't know the date for certain — things like that were easy to lose track of when you were on the move — but he didn't think they had used up all of August yet. Just the same, it was always winter at the elevation they were ascending, where wind whipped the snowy peaks with hurricane force, dragging thin, wispy snow clouds across the sky.

When they achieved the ridge, they reined in at the top of the world where tempest winds drove spicules of ice against their blankets and coats. Back where they had come from, Buena Vista was less than a smudge on the valley floor. And beyond it to the east, the mountains rolled like waves, rising one after the other toward the white-topped cone of Pike's Peak, at the very eastern edge of the Rocky Mountains.

To the west the land fell away, but less so than where they had come from. Pitkin was down there someplace, in one of those valleys down below the tree line, protected from the chill teeth that bit through their clothing here at the top.

They started down again. The trees closed back in around them and late summer returned. Coats and blankets came off. That afternoon they drew rein in a grove of quaking aspen at the head of a valley that opened up below to embrace the town. The long echoing moan of a train whistle signaled their return to civilization and Neville Hallidae grinned as he stepped up on a rock and stretched back his hand at Ben.

Ben lowered the spyglass through which he'd been studying the town, and handed it up to Neville. Neville glassed the valley, then turned to survey the rising mountains around it. He steadied the glass on a spot, then handed it back to Ben.

"There. We'll make camp up there," he

said, stepping up into his saddle. They rode back up the valley a mile to a high meadow beyond sight of Pitkin. Across the valley the mountain climbed toward the gray saddle of rock they had crossed over earlier. Ben watched the late-afternoon sun play across its barren face in shifting hues of salmon-colored light. Windblown snow off the higher peaks obscured the ridge, like a thin bridal veil.

Andy hopped to the ground and immediately discovered the tines of a deer antler poking up through the grass and wildflowers. She wrestled it free and carried it back to show Ben. A grove of aspen ringed the meadow, and the thinnest trickle of a cold stream cut back and forth through the tall grass.

Neville said, "Ben will come with me while we still have daylight. You make camp here." He narrowed an eye at Tom, then caught Turner Wilson in the same tight look. "You two keep off of each other's throats, hear me?" His glance touched Scott Mcintyre briefly, and then he looked away. He said to Turner, "Keep your hands off the kid. I don't want no trouble here while we're gone. Ben and I will check out the bank and be back around dark. Tomorrow we'll go in quick and afterward disappear before that marshal has any idea we've been here."

"Uncle Ben?"

Ben glanced at Andy. She held up the antler in one hand, the other filled with red and purple flowers for him to see. "I found it over there," she said.

"That's nice," he said, distracted, and swung up into his saddle.

"Are you going somewhere?" she asked, suddenly worried.

"Neville and I need to ride into town for a while."

"Can I go with you?"

"No," Neville said flatly.

She looked at Ben with eyes that pleaded with him not to leave her. A pang of sympathy shot through Ben. Ten years ago another little girl had asked almost the same question, and he had given the same answer. "It will be best if you stay, Andy," he said. But without conviction.

"But I don't want to." Her eyes flicked back to Turner Wilson.

Tom came up and dropped a hand onto her shoulder. "Old Tom will watch over you, chil'," he said in his deep voice. He peered at Ben and said, "Don't worry 'bout her."

Ben nodded his head. "I'll be back, Andy," he said and turned his horse away.

Pitkin was everything Alpine had not been. A town with an air of permanence. Its buildings stood straight and proud, bright in the afternoon sunlight as if their inhabitants truly cared about them. The streets were wide and bordered with straight, level sidewalks. The sign at the edge of town as they had entered gave the population at twenty-five hundred people, and Ben could believe it, for its streets were every bit as busy as Alpine's street had been.

There was no way to count them all, but Ben guessed there might be a hundred businesses in Pitkin, all booming, most having something to do with the affairs of mining. They turned in at the hitching rail in front of the clapboard bank building and stepped safely over the mud to the boardwalk. The air was heavy with the pungent odor of manure mixed with mud. One enjoys that peculiar aroma only after a hearty rainstorm such as they had endured the day before.

Inside, Neville immediately went to a wide table where three other men stood scribbling numbers on bank slips. He dipped a pen into the inkwell and glanced around as he put it to paper and pretended to write.

Ben studied the windows protected behind iron bars. He eyed the uniformed constable standing near the doorway. Three tellers worked the window behind bars painted sky blue. There was no safe in sight, but a door behind the teller box had strong iron-bar gates, which were presently opened inward and flat against the wall.

This place posed a bit more of a problem than the depository at Buena Vista, but it was not overly burdensome. The guard could be handled in a quiet and expedient manner. Someone would have to hurry through the back offices to make certain no danger remained there, but they had worked it that way before.

Ben felt a surge of excitement as he measured the distance from the door to the teller windows with his eyes. He viewed the single front door and the big windows. The traffic out front worried him some, but the windows had curtains that could be drawn, and once they were back outside, the glut of people would work to their advantage.

Then he thought about Andy, and the fire of excitement died like the light of a candle suddenly snuffed. She would not approve. But why should he care anyway? He didn't know, but just the same, he'd lost the heady enthusiasm that planning a job like this had once brought.

Neville wadded up the paper and tossed it

into a metal pail. "Seen enough?" he asked in a low voice.

"Yeah."

Outside, Neville glanced along the street. "We'll tie up our horses right here. Too many folks around to chance it any other way. We'll leave the mule at the camp. I got a feeling we'll need to give ourselves plenty of room for a fast run if need be. Damn busy place," he said, and lines of worry wrinkled his forehead.

"Maybe we ought to forget it, Neville."

Neville came around with a worried look in his eyes.

Ben grinned. "We got plenty of money to last us to Idaho, and then some."

"You've changed, Ben. Used to be the bigger the challenge, the more you went after it."

"I haven't changed," Ben said, trying to sound unconcerned. "It's just with that marshal somewhere back there, I'd breathe a lot easier if we were already on our way to someplace else."

Neville regarded him a moment longer. "No. That's not it," he said thoughtfully. "I haven't figured it out yet, but that's not it."

Ben laughed. "You're getting jumpy."

Neville pursed his lips, and kept his thoughts to himself. "It's time to leave, Ben."

"Not just yet. Something I need to buy first." Ben looked along the street.

"Buy?"

"Yep, and there is the place that just might sell it," Ben said, walking off.

Twenty-four

"This is getting us nowhere, Marshal. I say we go back to where we lost their trace in the first place and start all over again."

Devon had been studying the face of a gray and umber granite cliff that soared precipitously just beyond the blue spruce clinging to the mountainside around which wound the game trail they'd been following. The faint odor of chimney smoke rose from the valley below, where Landy's map showed the town of Alpine. Devon was thinking it would be his next stop in his search for Neville Hallidae.

The marshal slid around in his saddle. The effort of the last few days pulled heavily at the line that radiated from his eyes and stretched below his dark cheeks. He considered Franklin Dean, his expression hooded beneath the broad brown hat. "You do as you please, Dean. I have no authority over you. Only keep in mind that whatever trail there was has been rained on. You'll find yourself no better off than you are now." Devon inclined his head toward the valley to his right. "Down there somewhere is a town. It's likely we'll have word on Hallidae there, and perhaps on your little girl, too."

Dean rocked back in his saddle, his frown deepening, but he agreed that, for the moment, checking out the town was the next logical way to proceed.

Devon glanced at the haggard expressions on his deputies' faces as they slouched in their saddles. Without thinking about it, he drew himself up straighter and squared his wide shoulders. You don't grow old allowing life to beat you down, was his philosophy, and Walter Devon had every intention of growing old.

"If you gentlemen are ready?" he said, turning back, "then we'll . . ." Devon's words broke off. He squinted ahead and nudged his horse off the trail to the left until the trees stopped him.

"What is it?" Landy asked, coming instantly out of his saddle fatigue.

Devon steadied his horse near a tall spruce and stood in the stirrups, stretching his six-foot four-inch frame to its limits. He reached up into the branches, fished around a bit, and sat back in his saddle holding a rag doll in his hand.

Franklin Dean's eyes expanded when he saw it. "Susie Meyers!"

Devon glanced at the tattered and shredded doll — more of its stuffing missing than remaining. Franklin Dean spurred his horse ahead and drew rein almost at once by Devon's side.

"That's Susie Meyers," he said, trembling with excitement.

"It's only a doll," Devon said.

"It's Andoreana's doll!" Dean grabbed it away, and as he looked it over, his excitement turned to agonizing concern. "Andoreana would never leave it behind, Marshal. Something terrible has happened to her! Look — look how it has been cut up!"

Devon glanced at the tree where he'd extracted the doll, and slowly his eyes traveled up to the cliff he'd been studying a moment before. "Up there," he said. "It came from up there."

The horses struck sparks as their hooves glanced off the hard rock in the scrambling climb. On top were the signs of a recent camp.

"I told you, Marshal. I told you they had taken my Andoreana," Franklin Dean was raving, his words rambling and disjointed as he walked around the campsite at a frantic pace, accomplishing nothing.

Devon put the excited man out of mind and concentrated on the signs Hallidae had left behind for him. The recent rains made their trace plain, and Devon constructed a picture of what had happened here.

They'd pitched dog tents, and the dry rectangles of ground showed Devon exactly where they'd pitched them. The campfire was dead. Devon stuck his hand in the earth beneath the gray ash. They'd ridden in from the south. Later two horses had left the camp, and then returned. The hoofprints had been mostly washed away by the storm, but over here were the new tracks made in fresh mud, leaving the camp by the north. Five horses and a mule. Tracks pressed deep in the soft earth.

Plain as San Francisco Street through the middle of Santa Fe! Devon's fist tightened with renewed energy. This was a new hand, dealt suddenly by the help of a rag doll, and most welcome.

Landy found two more cigarette butts, and he couldn't have been happier if he had plucked up a pair of newly minted double eagles.

"We've got them now, Marshal," Landy said with no trace of his earlier boredom.

Hedstrom rode in from the direction Neville Hallidae had left the camp. "Hallidae is heading west, all right."

Devon eyed the angry gray mountain peaks to the west where the sturdy pine and spruce of the lower elevations could not survive. If Hallidae was up there, Devon would follow.

Like it or not, he'd follow the man into hell if need be. He gathered up his reins and swung back onto his horse.

"Hallidae left here this morning," he said. "There is still warmth beneath their fire pit, and these tracks are only hours old. We do some hard riding now, we can close the distance." Devon rested his big hand on the ivory handle of his revolver and studied the snow clouds teased off the mountaintops by the winds at fourteen thousand feet. Well, it had to be done, and he heard no complaints as the others swung up into their saddles.

Then Devon spied something trampled into the ground. He stepped down and pulled the remains of a small nightgown from the stiffening mud.

"My God," Franklin Dean said. "What have they done to her?"

"Ye be trimming the wicks now and filling them before dark." McKormick glanced at his watch and tucked it back into his vest pocket. "The evening is coming on and I don't want anyone running into the merchandise."

"Yes, sir, Mr. McKormick." The afternoon had been slow, and the lack of customers had done little to humor the proprietor. Kathleen knew her prompt reply was all that Kelvin McKormick required or even wanted; not a complaint that she was already occupied sweeping the floors, as he had requested only five minutes earlier, and that she would see to the lamps when she was finished.

McKormick kept the coal oil in a jug outside the back door. Kathleen set the broom against the door jamb, and as she went back through the storage room, she was alerted to incoming customers by the bell out front. But Whithers was there, as was the assayer, Reading, and even the *Lord of the Manor* himself. She hauled in the heavy jug, setting it upon a table where McKormick had instructed that the lamps were to be filled. McKormick was, however, the owner of this store, and if she did not like the way he ran his business or treated his employees, it was up to her to seek employment elsewhere.

She set out a funnel and a sharp pair of wick scissors, and went back out front for the first lamp. Scarcely had she stepped through the doorway than she stopped as if having walked into an invisible wall. She heaved in a startled breath and her eyes widened. The man Whithers was talking to was the very same man who had taken her money in Buena Vista. Kathleen Hamil was certain. Dark hair, bushy mustache, hollowed cheeks beneath the prominent rise of his cheekbones. She wanted to cry out but stifled the urge.

The man with him was shorter, and she recognized the hat and shirt — the one who had barked the orders during the robbery!

She stood frozen in the doorway a moment, then got her wits about her and ducked back behind the door. Whithers was saying, "Yes, I think we have just what you are looking for. Right back this way."

She heard their footsteps come nearer. Then they were right on the other side of the wall, right where McKormick kept the items children wanted.

"Here, this is what I'm looking for," she heard the man say. There was no doubt that the voice was the same, too.

"It's one of our most popular items," Whithers said encouragingly. "For your daughter?"

Kathleen heard the fleeting hesitation before the bank robber spoke. "Yes, my daughter. She has been asking for a doll just like this. I'll take it."

"Very good. If you will just step this way, I shall wrap it up for you."

Their footsteps moved away. Kathleen chanced a peek around the door frame. By the counter, the outlaw was digging coins from his vest pocket while the other man glanced warily about. She pulled back as his eyes swept past. Then she heard the crinkle of brown paper being bundled up, and Mr. Whithers thanking the outlaw again.

When the door struck the bell and slammed shut, Kathleen burst from the back room. She reached under the counter for her hat and tied the ribbon under her chin as she stepped to the window. Her breath came in quick spurts, and she felt her heart pounding. They were walking down the sidewalk. They were getting away! She headed for the door.

"Where do ye think ye are going, Mrs. Hamil?"

McKormick's voice hit her like a fist out of the dark and she leaped around, startled.

"Those men . . . those two men. They're —"

"I said, where are ye going?" He tapped his toe impatiently, peering sharply at her over his spectacles and past his pinched nose.

"To see the sheriff, of course. To see Harlan Geckhorn. I have to tell him —"

"Geckhorn has not been here making his rounds," McKormick said, interrupting her again. He didn't seem to understand what she was trying to tell him.

Her impatience flared. "I must see the sheriff."

"Ye are not excused from your work yet, Mrs. Hamil, and ye may not leave here to visit your sheriff friend until I give ye leave.

Now, remove that bonnet and get ye back to the lamps."

"I will not."

He turned and considered her narrowly.

"Ye will, Madam."

Kathleen Hamil put her hand on the door-knob and felt strangely elated. "I will not, sir. I will not, for I quit!"

She pulled the door open and was gone.

Twenty-five

Ben and Neville found their way back to the camp by the light of the fire that danced upon the gray trunks of quaking aspen.

Ben swung down and immediately searched for Andy. He discovered the child sitting near the fire upon a blanket with half of it drawn up over her shoulders. Her smile, when she saw him striding across the dark ground toward her, told Ben she had not been bothered further by Turner.

"Take care of your business, Uncle Ben?"

"Yep."

She lowered her voice. "You going to rob another bank?"

Ben leveled a warning stare at the child, "Keep those thoughts to yourself, Andy."

"I know." She hesitated as if wanting to say more, then fell into a grim quietness as she stared at the flames. The last of the elk meat that Mcintyre had shot the day before was cooking on a spit.

Ben poured himself a cup of coffee.

"Uncle Ben?" she said suddenly.

"Hum?" He sensed that same reluctance in her voice.

"Yesterday I . . . I guess I forgot and let it slip to that Mr. Wilson that I know you all are bank robbers." She looked up lamely. "I'm sorry."

Ben cradled the coffee cup in both hands and considered the implications of what Andy had said. Across the way Neville was unfurling his long canvas ground sheet. Turner Wilson came out of the darkness and Neville and he fell into a quiet conversation. Did Hallidae know? He hadn't mentioned it.

"Neville thought it might come out. He didn't guess five men on the move, two steps ahead of the law and looking to build up a kitty along the way, was something we could long keep from a bright tyke like you."

"I'm not a tyke."

Ben gave her a grin.

"What will he do?"

"I don't know, Andy, but this might not be a bad time for you and me to keep our eyes open." Ben handed her the brown paper bundle he'd brought with him.

"What is this?"

"Open it up."

Andy looked at the package a moment. "Cut the strings, Uncle Ben."

He opened his pocket knife. "Here, you do it."

Andy cut the strings carefully, and as the

paper fell away, her eyes widened and a smile came to her face. "It's a doll!"

"To replace Susie Meyers."

Her smile faltered and she said, "Thank you, but I can never replace Susie Meyers."

"Don't you like it?"

"Oh, yes," Andy said, but Ben sensed that her enthusiasm had waned. Maybe it was just that the little girl in her had grown up so much in the last several days. *Maybe she's outgrown dolls,* he thought. "Thank you," she said.

"What are you gonna name her?"

"I don't know yet. I'll have to think about it."

"Well, names are important. It's best you give it some thought." He left her then, going to his saddle. Setting his coffee cup on a rock, he untied his bedroll and pulled the saddle off his horse.

Mcintyre dragged in a deadfall limb and went after it with a hatchet. As his chopping echoed in the darkness, Tom Deveraux was suddenly at Ben's side.

"What do you think those two are talking about?"

Ben glanced over. Turner and Neville were having an earnest talk, but Ben could not hear a word of it. He took that as ominous, for they were not twenty feet off, and anything but a guarded conversation would reach his ears.

In turn, Tom spoke softly, too. "Ya know, Ben, there is something cookin' between them two. I don't like it."

Ben took up his coffee cup and tasted the cooling liquid in it. "Turner is stirring things up," he said.

"It's more'n that."

"You mean Andy?"

"I mean Andy. And me, too. Wilson and me, we never did get on mighty good. And after the last few days, well, it's about to come to blood, Ben."

Ben had been suspecting that for over a year, watching the two of them lock horns. In the beginning, it seemed no more than playful bantering between the two of them. But gradually Ben watched it grow serious. Wilson did not like the black man, and he made no bones about it. Ben decided that Turner Wilson did not really like any of them, only it was Tom he most resented.

"What are you going to do?"

Tom shrugged his shoulders. "I could take him on if'n I wanted. A little fellow like that, I could break in two . . . if'n I wanted."

"If you wanted?"

Tom gave a short laugh. "It's funny, but since that kid has come among us, I've been doing some serious thinking about what I'm doing — I mean, doing here. I never wanted this. Not really. It's something I sort of drifted into."

"Andy has had that same effect on me."

Tom laughed. "Can you imagine us, grow'd-up men, saying a meal prayer?"

"I wouldn't have thought it," Ben said, giving Tom a grin. Then he turned serious. "Don't underestimate Turner. He's small, but he's got instinct. He kills because he enjoys it. If you have to go up against him, make sure his hands are empty. He'll never take you empty-handed. I don't know that I could say the same if he gets hold of that big knife he carries."

Tom nodded his head, and took his thoughts back with him to his bedroll, where he sat in the shadows.

Harlan Geckhorn rapped his desk with the horseshoe paperweight. "All right, quiet down!" he ordered. The tumult died down to a few desultory remarks, and then to quietness as the sheriff gathered their attention.

His command over these men impressed Kathleen Hamil. This same man who was so nervous in McKormick's store was truly in control here.

"All right, now, I told you what Mrs. Hamil

has told me. They were the very men who held up the bank in Buena Vista. Now they show up here in Pitkin. That says to me they are up to no good. And you, Virgil, you say you saw them in the bank?" Geckhorn stabbed a finger at one of the faces in the crowd.

The fellow named Virgil stammered, suddenly intimidated by the men who looked to him now. "Well, they sure did fit the description that the lady gave," he said. "I filled out my deposit right there next to the one she says is their leader." His voice grew bolder. "Why, if I had known, I would have —"

"It's a good thing you didn't know, Virgil," Harlan said, cutting him short, "or there would have been bloodshed for certain."

"Ah, I suppose so, sheriff," Virgil melted back into the comfortable oblivion of the mob. Kathleen watched as another man stepped forward.

"If it is true, if these are the same men, this Neville . . . Hallidae?" The speaker glanced at her for affirmation and she nodded her head. "Then what are we going to do about it, sheriff?"

"That's precisely why I called you here this evening," Geckhorn said. It amazed Kathleen how Geckhorn had mastered the crowd with a confidence that comes naturally only to a few men. He was in his environment here.

"I've gone through the posters with Mrs. Hamil. She has definitely identified the two of them, so the only conclusion I can come to is they intend to rob our bank. My guess is, they came in this afternoon to look the place over. Tomorrow, most likely morning, they'll make their try."

A wave of agreement swept through the room and washed over Harlan Geckhorn. He silenced them with a hand and said, "Now, I intend to deputize as many men as I need."

Instantly arms went up and a clangor of "Ayes" and "Me," issued forth from the crowd.

"And then," Geckhorn said above their noise, "we'll be ready for them come the morrow."

The horses picked their way through the darkness as the riders huddled down in their coats against the icy winds driving relentlessly against them. Neville Hallidae's trace had disappeared with the coming of night, but the horses saw plain enough the trail worn into the barren ground. There was no place else Neville Hallidae could have gone but along this game track, up over the saddle of rock that they approached now, black against the night sky.

It would be inconvenient to set up camp

here where the winds howled and no firewood could be found. And even if fuel could be located, starting a fire in this thin air would certainly present a challenge. So Devon drove on through the night, battered by the wind but not by his deputies, who seemed renewed in their energy now that Hallidae's trace had been found again.

By midnight they had crossed over the crest of the saddle and descended back into the trees where Devon finally drew up. Wearily, they threw out their bedrolls and crawled in without the benefit of a fire, or any food other than the peanuts they had eaten until the sack was near empty. Despite this, they were immediately asleep.

Almost at once Devon found himself rousted out of his stiff blankets. A screeching jay warmed itself in a patch of light where morning sun piercing the ridge above climbed down the face of a tall ponderosa pine.

They boiled coffee and fried bacon, and Tom opened a can of peaches and passed them around for the men and Andy to fork out. Breakfast was eaten in a hostile silence that boded no good. Neville was particularly pensive, avoiding Ben's eye as he ate. He'd come to a decision during the night. He wished it hadn't been necessary to make it, but it was necessary to ensure his own security in the days ahead.

Neville paced a couple hundred yards from the camp and stood at the head of the valley, looking west. This would be the way they'd make their departure in the minutes of confusion that follow a holdup. He glanced at the men by the campfire, then studied the gray, windswept chain of mountain peaks now to their east. With the Continental Divide now behind him, he had an easy avenue of flight out of this country, while those forbidding peaks remained a barrier to Devon. Neville wasn't worried about the marshal, though. It was pursuit from the town below that would be his main concern, and therefore, he laid out his avenue of escape with that in mind.

When he had it fixed in his memory, Neville caught the eye of Turner Wilson and gave him a nod of his head. Wilson shoved his hands deep into his pockets and kicked through the stiff, brown grass.

"What you got on your mind, Neville?"

Neville turned his back to the camp. He said, "You notice a change come over Ben of late?"

"Since we picked up the kid?"

"Then, and maybe a little before."

"He's gotten soft. I don't know what it is, Neville, only, I wouldn't want to count on him if I needed someone to cover for me."

Neville nodded his head and studied the peaks of the Collegiate Mountain Range they had crossed the day before. He said, "That's what I've been thinking. And I've been thinking something else. I think the time has come to end our association with Ben, and with Tom, too. If you ask me, those two are up to no good as far as the rest of us are concerned. I wouldn't doubt but they are planning to cut and run on us, and maybe take all that we have worked hard to get."

Neville got the response he'd baited Turner for. He saw it in Turner's suddenly angry eyes. He said, "Not now. We'll bide our time. After we've finished with this morning's chore and are safely away from Pitkin, then we'll move on Ben, and Tom."

Turner's outrage eased into a grin. "That will leave us with bigger cuts."

"One of the benefits of paring down our numbers. Besides, three men will be harder to follow than five."

"And the kid?"

"That kid would finger us in a minute."

"Let me do it."

"No. Not your way."

"If I make it fast?"

Neville looked at him, considering. "All right. Only, don't take pleasure in it."

Turner's grin widened. "Anything you say, Neville."

"One more thing." Neville caught Turner by the sleeve as the other man had begun to turn away. "Pass it on to Mcintyre. Tell him if he sticks with us, he's in. If not . . ." Neville raised his eyebrows speculatively. "Come on, it's time to get moving."

Twenty-six

"We'll be back shortly, Andy," Ben said as they mounted up. Andy nodded her head but didn't reply, as if denying what they were planning on doing would somehow prevent it. Ben grimaced as Andy hitched the new doll under her arm and found a place to sit beneath the aspens.

They were all going down to Pitkin, except Tom. Neville had instructed the black man to stay with Andy and to see that they were ready to move once the four of them returned. Neville turned his horse away and Ben, Scott, and Turner followed him.

Ben considered the way his life had gone since joining up with Hallidae. It hadn't been a bad life, but it was nothing he was proud of. He remembered Tom saying he'd not want his family to see how he turned out. Ben felt the same now as he rode away from the camp, and Andy. He thought of the reluctance he felt in Alpine. He didn't want to rob that bank then, and he was relieved when they didn't have to. And here he was, planning to do it all over again.

Some men can't change, he told himself,

realizing bitterly that he was one of them.

Pitkin was a bright painted gem on the mountainside in the morning sun as they descended toward the town. They rode up the wide dirt street and turned into the hitching rail along the sidewalk one storefront away from the bank.

The town had seemed somehow different to Ben today.

He stepped up to the sidewalk and studied the long street, with its side streets branching off to more businesses and the homes beyond. Ben discovered he was staring at a nearly empty sidewalk, and hardly any traffic on the street. Ben had lost track of the days and he was beginning to wonder if it wasn't Sunday and everyone was off in church. But no, the bank doors were open wide, as if calling them inside.

"We all know what to do," Neville said, bringing Ben's attention back to the task at hand. Just the same, a nagging uneasiness lingered in the back of his brain.

They had talked the plan out on their ride down, each man given an assignment. Turner was to attach himself to the guard a moment after the rest of them entered, pulling up his mask at the last moment. No one would take particular notice to him before they began, and afterward a half-dozen descriptions would surely conflict, Hallidae had told them.

Scott was to make his way immediately back to the offices and roust anyone there out where they could be watched. Ben would pull the shades and then oversee the extraction of the bank's funds while Hallidae orchestrated the affair, making certain no one caused trouble.

"Ben, you got something to say?"

Ben apparently had been frowning. "Seems quiet, Neville. Where did everyone go?"

Neville glanced at a clock down the street above a watchmaker's shop. "It's early. Maybe the place doesn't wake up till after noon." He grinned then at Ben. "Don't look so worried. It will make getting away all that much easier."

Ben nodded his head. "I suppose," he said. But just the same, an uneasiness had come over him that was not the usual tenseness that precedes a holdup.

Neville glanced at Wilson. "You go in now. Remember, wait until Scott is in place and I step in."

Wilson turned up the collar of his duster and went inside the bank.

Neville looked at Ben, concerned. "You ready, Ben?"

Ben Masters loosened the revolver in its holster. He gave the town a quick glance. It was just too quiet. *Too damn quiet.* "I'm ready, Neville."

Neville said to Scott, "Get in place."

Mcintyre disappeared into the bank, and it was only Ben and Neville out on the sidewalk.

"Here goes," Neville said, moving toward the tall bank door. He gave Ben a grin and then covered it with his mask.

Ben lingered a moment longer on the door-step, his eyes moving swiftly along the empty sidewalk. Then he spied movement on a roof-top across the street, caught a glimpse of the face of a man up there. Instantly an alarm sounded in his brain, but it was too late to back out now. He pulled up his mask, drew his revolver, and stepped inside the bank.

"There it is, Marshal," Franklin Dean said all at once, his words bursting forth like an explosion. His finger shook with a release of pent-up worry at the tracks in the pine needle litter.

Walt Devon swung off his horse and knelt down by the trail. They had lost it during the night, and had spent the first hour of the morning scanning the ground for it. But Devon hadn't been as concerned as Franklin Dean. Devon had traced Neville Hallidae across desert, river, and barren mountainsides. He had closed the distance between him and the outlaw to less than a day, and he knew his search was nearing an end. Devon hadn't worried over the dark throwing him off Hallidae's trace. The dark was not his adversary. Neville Hallidae was, and the outlaw leader wasn't making any effort to hide his passage. What was lost in the night would easily be found again in the day.

But Franklin Dean fretted with a father's concern — the ability to think logically had fled the man.

Devon stepped back into his saddle and pulled himself up straight on the tall horse. The craggy relief of his sun-darkened face beneath the wide brown hat revealed none of his own excitement. He said, "Gentlemen, we will have Neville Hallidae against the ropes by noon, if I judge correctly. Dean, you ever go up against a man?"

Franklin Dean hesitated, then said, "No, Marshal. Not with a gun. But I've whipped a few with my bare fist," he went on with boldness coming into his voice.

Devon considered the father a moment, then turned a hard face on Landy and Hedstrom. "And you two?"

Regrettably, they both had to admit that they had never done any more than escort drunks and bullies into the Chaffee County Jail. Chaffee County had its share of rough and bawdy miners and saloons, but it was sadly lacking in hard-core criminals.

"That's what I thought," Devon said, rocking back in his saddle. "Well, I suppose you all know how to use those irons you're packing?"

They gave an enthusiastic response to that, as if a hearty "yea" would make amends of a life of little adventure.

Devon frowned. After all, he had asked the governor to supply him with only two deputies; he hadn't specified hardened lawmen. And he hadn't gotten any either.

"Well, you three are liable to get an education today. There isn't much I can tell you that five minutes of experience won't teach you better. But I'll advise you this much: keep your heads down when you can, and keep your wits about you. When the bullets start to fly, most men stop thinking and start shooting. You do it the other way around and you'll make out."

From the window in the sheriff's office, Kathleen Hamil watched Ben and Neville enter the bank. "They are the same men, all right," she said. "The ones who robbed the bank in Buena Vista."

"Here, now, you get away from that window, Mrs. Hamil," Harlan said, taking her gently but firmly by the arm. She came away without a fuss.

He sat her down in a chair in a corner, on the far side of a heavy oak filing cabinet between her and the window. Harlan said she'd be safe from stray bullets there. It seemed logical to her, and so gallant for the sheriff to consider her safety.

From her chair she watched Geckhorn's self-assured authority over the men that he'd deputized the night before, and she had a difficulty calling to mind the bumbling image of the man who stopped by McKormick's store.

How odd, she thought.

Once the outlaws were inside the bank, Geckhorn stepped out of his office and began directing the men up and down the street. He stuck his head back inside and said to her, "Now you stay put, Mrs. Hamil."

"Yes," she said, but the moment he was gone she leaped from the chair and pressed her nose against the windowpane. She could see them placed where Harlan directed — atop the buildings, standing in the shadows, and looking around corners. And then she saw Harlan Geckhorn climb the sidewalk across the street. He carried himself with a confidence that up until now Kathleen Hamil had noticed only in her deceased husband, George.

She watched Harlan carry his Winchester rifle into Bailey's Millinery Shop, only two doors down from the bank.

And then she, like the rest of the town, waited.

Twenty-seven

Neville closed and barred the bank door. Turner already had the guard at gunpoint and Scott came out of the last door at the rear of the building with the thin-faced man in a gray suit under his gun.

"No one else back there," Mcintyre said.

Neville motioned with his revolver. "Put the gent over there with the guard."

"See here —" the man protested.

"Shut up," Mcintyre barked, shoving the older gentleman up against the wall alongside the bank guard.

Turner kept them both covered while Mcintyre jumped to help Ben draw the shades.

Ben spent a moment peering out into the street. He spied a second man lingering around a corner with a rifle in hand. His thoughts raced ahead, working on the problem as he heard Hallidae's voice saying, "You folks know what this is all about. I don't guess I need to threaten you none 'cause you already know if you try anything daring you'll end up a corpse. Any questions?"

There were no questions, mainly, Ben figured, because there were so few folks in the bank to ask them. Only one teller, the president, and the guard. There had been three tellers the day before — and customers aplenty.

Neville glanced at Ben and motioned him toward the teller's window. Ben ignored him for the moment and said to Mcintyre, "Did you see a back door?"

"There is one."

"Make sure it's barred."

Mcintyre went to check. Ben noticed Neville's impatient scowl. He stepped up beside the outlaw leader and spoke near his ear. "We got problems, Neville. There are armed men out front on the roofs and along the side streets."

Neville moved alongside a window and peeked around the curtains. "Shit!" he said, turning back to the empty room.

"What is it?" Turner asked.

Neville ignored the question and said to Ben, "Let's finish what we are here for."

Ben nodded and hurried the teller down the hallway to where he found a vault with its doors opened. On the floor were half a dozen canvas bags, sewn shut at the top, with the words DENVER MINT stenciled across them in bold letters and the figure 20,000 in smaller numbers beneath. Ben directed the teller to gather up two of them, and he took two more under his arm.

Back out in the main room, Ben cut a hole in the top seam of each bag and tied a rope between two sacks, making them into convenient parcels to toss over their saddles. He handed a pair of bags to Scott, and the second pair he slung over his shoulder.

"What's goin' on?" Turner glanced anxiously over his shoulder at Hallidae, who had taken up a post by the window where he could keep an eye on the street.

Ben said, "We've been found out. There are armed men all up and down the street just waiting for us to step out."

"Damn!" he said, and he licked his lips. "What we gonna do?"

Ben grabbed the startled bank president by the sleeve and hauled him over to Hallidae. Neville turned from the window. "I've spotted six." His voice was taut, but under control.

Ben said, "We only have one way out of here."

Neville looked at him.

Ben nodded at the pale man he had by the arm. "We make a deal."

Neville played the idea over in his head then agreed.

Ben said to the man, "How many men are there out there?"

"I don't know what you're talking about —"

Ben's revolver came up and nested just below the man's ribs.

"About ten or twelve!"

"And who is in charge?"

"The sheriff — Harlan Geckhorn."

Ben glanced at Neville. "He's the one we need to talk to."

Neville nodded and shoved the wooden bar off the door. Ben pulled it open a crack and looked outside. The street was deserted now, as if a barricade had been thrown up on either side. There were faces in many of the windows but not a soul out of doors anywhere. *A clever trap,* Ben thought wryly, and they had walked easily into it. How could they have known? Was Devon somehow responsible? He couldn't imagine how.

Ben shouted, "Geckhorn — I want to talk to you."

For a moment his words seemed to hang in the air, unanswered. Then a voice came back at him from somewhere down the street.

"I'm Geckhorn. What can I do for you boys?" The voice had an easy, confident quality about it, as if the person behind it was actually enjoying the proceedings.

Ben glanced at Neville, then at the bank president, and said, "We got us a hostage here,

Geckhorn. If you don't want a dead bank president, you'll call off your men and let us leave."

The voice came back. "You can leave anytime you want. But the money stays in the bank."

Neville pushed past Ben and put his face near the door. "No deal, Geckhorn. We take the money with us. And we take this man, too. Anyone starts shooting, he gets it first."

There was a long pause and finally Geckhorn said, "Have it your way, boys."

Ben said, "And he gets it if we see anyone following us, too."

"No one will follow. You boys are free to go."

Ben glanced at Neville. "He's making it too easy."

Neville looked worried too. "Maybe he knows we got him over a barrel."

"We?"

"He doesn't want anyone getting hurt," Neville shot back angrily.

"I don't like this, not one bit."

Neville glared at him, the strain showing. "What the hell other choice do we have?"

Regrettably, Ben could think of none. He saw a horse tied a short distance away and hauled the president around in front of his gun. He said to Neville, "I'll get that horse

for him. Then we will all leave. Warn Mcintyre and Turner not to do anything stupid.
As long as we don't start shooting, I don't
think they will."

Ben pulled the president around in front of
him and, with the gun in his back, stepped
out onto the sidewalk. The morning sun stung
his eyes. He eased the man toward the horse
tied nearby. Men crowded the windows, and
guns bristled everywhere. Ben settled his
nerves, reminding himself that as long as they
knew he meant to kill his hostage at the first
indication of attack, he was safe. Just the same,
Ben moved the barrel of his revolver to the
bank president's head where everyone could
see it.

They untied the horse and brought the animal to where the others were tied. One by
one, Neville Hallidae and the others stepped
out. Ben motioned for the man to mount up
and followed swiftly into his own saddle, never
allowing his revolver to stray for one moment
from its target. The others slung the money
bags over their saddles and mounted up. Neville raised his voice to the deserted street.
"Anyone tries to follow, this man is dead."
He put his own revolver on the prisoner, and
they started out of town.

Harlan Geckhorn stepped out and watched

them break into a gallop at the edge of town. He was grinning when one of the men he'd deputized came up.

"What now, sheriff?"

Geckhorn said, "We give them some time like they asked." His grin widened. "We wouldn't want Neville Hallidae to get the idea that this is how we planned it now, would we, Frank?"

"No, reckon not, sheriff." Geckhorn could tell that Frank wasn't all that convinced it had gone as planned, after all.

"Besides, wouldn't want old Mr. Stevenson to get hurt now, would we?"

Frank shook his head.

The teller and the guard emerged from the bank just then, their faces regaining a healthy glow. The teller said, "They took the bags, just like you said they would, sheriff. Didn't even touch the money in the drawers, or the vault."

"Well, that's what we wanted. The bank's money is safe and Hallidae got what he wanted. Now we can get us a posse together and confront the man out where we don't have to worry about any innocent bystanders getting hurt."

Geckhorn glanced at his watch. "Well, I'd say it's time for some breakfast. Frank, get the boys together. I'll be at my office seeing how Mrs. Hamil is. Then the lady and I will be over to Lucy's Café having a bite. When you're ready, give me a holler. We'll give Hallidae an hour or so to settle down, then go after him."

Twenty-eight

They dropped the bank president about a mile out of town and left him afoot. Ben had stepped in when Neville had drawn his revolver. "It makes no difference now," he'd said and Neville could see that Ben meant for the man to keep his life.

When they rode into camp, Tom could see that something had gone wrong; he told Andy to stay with the mule. Ben handed him the reins of the spare horse. "This is for Andy to ride," he said.

"What happened?"

"We nearly had to shoot our way out, and judging from the odds, we'd have never made it," Ben said.

Turner Wilson hauled a pair of money sacks over to a stump and put the point of his bowie to one of them.

"Tell me 'bout it."

Neville said, "It was a trap, Cotton. They knew we was coming."

"How could they know that?"

Neville shrugged his shoulders. "The local sheriff had it all figured out."

"Sheee-it!"

Neville stared a moment at Tom and Ben, then he said, "And that's not the half of it, Cotton. . . ."

"Neville!" Turner Wilson cried suddenly and wheeled toward the outlaw leader, his face white with shock. He held out the money sack he'd just cut open, and in his other hand a fistful of newsprint cut up and bundled together like bills fresh from the mint. Wilson flung the bogus money to the ground and slit open a second bag, dumping packages of newsprint at their feet.

"Fake! It's all fake!" Turner fairly screamed. He dove for the other bags and split them open, dumping newsprint into a pile. He heaved up his bowie and drove it violently into the side of a tree, his body shuddering with rage. He stomped around on the phony money, kicking the bundles across their campsite, damning them to hell and beyond. "They knew it all along, damn it all!" he seethed.

Andy came closer, curiously, and with the doll dangling from her left hand, she tugged Ben's sleeve. "I'm sorry you had trouble, Uncle Ben, but I'm happy you didn't steal their money after all."

Ben grinned down at the child, seeing the humor in it now, grinning even wider at the stomping, romping character cursing the paper that spread out across the ground. He noticed that Tom was enjoying it, too. He said, "I'm kind of glad we didn't manage it either, Andy."

Then Neville was looking at him. His eyes were hard, and it was only after a moment did Ben see the revolver in Neville Hallidae's hand. "That kind of thinking is just what's getting in the way here, Ben." His words were drawn tight as a fiddle string.

Ben glanced at Scott Mcintyre. Scott's Colt's Lightning came reluctantly from his holster.

"Turner!" Neville barked, getting his attention.

The rage settled like simmering water, and gradually Wilson gathered control of himself and seemed to understand what was happening.

"Uncle Ben?"

But Ben's focus was full on Hallidae.

Neville was saying, "This morning when you caught on to the trap, that was the way you used to be all the time. I could count on you. But lately you've grown unreliable. You've taken it upon yourself to cross me one too many times, Ben, and I'm dissolving our partnership right now."

"Neville," Tom started to say, but the weapon in Turner's hand leveled at him, cutting him short.

Neville said, "I'm afraid you've chosen

which side you want on, Cotton. The two of you, drop your gun belts and step away from them."

Ben said, "Tom and I won't try to stop you from leaving, Neville."

Neville said, "You still don't see it, do you? You didn't understand it in Buena Vista when you let that woman live. You didn't learn even now, when you stood up for that fellow we took from the bank. They're called witnesses — you leave them behind, they'll catch up with you later. It might not be this week, this month, this year even. But one of these days they will catch up, and you'll regret you didn't deal with the problem in the first place."

"I never regretted letting a man or woman live when it was in my power to do so, Neville."

Neville nodded his head as if he fully understood. "That's the difference between you and me, Ben. That's why I'm ending this partnership here and now. Off with those belts."

Ben and Tom unbuckled their gun belts and Neville motioned for them to step away from them. Ben eased back saying, "What about Andy?"

"The kid can cause as much harm to us, or you or Tom," Neville said.

Ben cast about the camp. He had to stall somehow, but he was running out of words to say. Neville was in a hurry to be on his way before a posse from Pitkin found its way to their camp. Ben widened the distance between him and the outlaw leader and looked at Mcintyre. "You in with Neville?"

Scott was not happy about it, but Ben saw that Mcintyre wasn't going to go against Hallidae or Wilson.

"I'm sticking with Hallidae," Mcintyre said.

Then Ben's searching glance hit upon the bowie knife Turner had left in the tree, now only two arms' lengths away.

Tom said, "Neville, you can do with me as you please. I come to expect that from most white men, but let the chil' be. You won't gain nothin' by killin' her, too. Please, let Andy be. She can find her way down to town and back to her papa. Besides, they already know who you are by this time. Killin' her gives you nothing."

"She's mine to kill," Wilson said. "Neville gave her to me."

"That's right," Neville said.

Ben watched Andy step back as Turner reached for her, her eyes riveted on the leering man.

"Neville, don't!" Tom pleaded.

The outlaw leader took his eyes from Ben for an instant, bringing his revolver down on the black man. In that moment Ben lunged for the bowie, pulling it free of the soft bark of the aspen tree. He wheeled, cocking the big knife over his shoulder. Ben was not as self-assured as Turner was at throwing a knife, but he'd experimented with it some in the past, and then there were all those hours as a boy, playing hit-the-rock off the palisades above the Missouri River.

The nearer target was Wilson, and Ben aimed for it. The blade flashed in the sunlight and struck Turner Wilson in the chest. But Ben had thrown it wrong. The knife hit on the flat with a solid thump that knocked Wilson off his feet.

Neville came around, leveling his revolver.

Ben dove, rolled, and snatched up his holster belt as Neville's first shot boomed through the valley. In a glance, Ben saw Tom diving for his own revolver. Ben fired, and missed. The outlaw leader returned fire, kicking up dirt into Ben's eyes.

From his left, Ben heard Tom's gun pop twice.

Turner was back on his feet, firing as he raced for cover of the trees. Ben drew a bead and squeezed off a shot that sent Wilson stumbling forward.

And in the middle of it all stood Andy, as if frozen to the ground, her arms and the doll held up around her head. Beyond her, Neville was taking aim. Ben swung around and fired. Neville's gun barked back as Ben thumbed the hammer for another shot.

Mcintyre's .38 Lightning spoke once in the higher voice that Ben recognized as belonging to a smaller bullet. Tom silenced it with a single shot from his .45.

A hot poker stung Ben's thigh. Ben blinked the sweat from his eyes and found Neville in his sights. But Neville was moving. Ben tracked him and suddenly discovered Andy beyond the top of his revolver. He let up on the trigger, rolled once, picked up his target fleeing toward the trees, and fired.

Neville stumbled to his knees, came around, and threw back two quick shots.

Andy seemed to be in his line of fire again, and Ben stood now and took his time as Neville pushed himself along the ground toward a rock large enough to hide behind. Ben fired and Neville shuddered in his tracks. Then he collapsed and didn't move again.

All at once the shooting stopped, and Ben stood there trying to see everything at once. Tom was picking himself off the ground — he was shaking, but appeared unhurt. Andy was planted in the middle of their camp as solid as a tree, her head still covered. Across the way, Scott Mcintyre lay in a heap, and Wilson was staring back at Ben with eyes wide and frozen in death. Neville had made it the farthest — almost to the rock.

"You all right, Tom?"

Tom nodded his head. "I think so."

Ben went to Andy. It hurt him to walk. When he looked, he discovered a bloody furrow that parted the skin of his thigh. The girl was stiff as a board when he got to her. Ben pried her arms away from her head and knelt beside the child.

"It's all over, Andy."

She was shaking, and couldn't speak at first.

"It's all right," Ben soothed. "They won't hurt you."

Andy managed to say, "Are you hurt?"

"Just a nick. I'm okay."

She glanced suddenly at Tom. He gave her a wry grin, his revolver dangling at his side. "I'm all right, too, chil'."

Ben stared at the doll she'd been clutching. Cotton batting had been torn from it. Some of it covered Andy's shoulder. He looked Andy over closely, but the bullet that had passed through the doll had not touched her. Ben pulled her to him and gave her a hug. "We are all okay, now."

"That may be a bit premature, Ben," Tom said.

He was pointing at the valley that they had come through yesterday after crossing the Divide. Ben squinted against the sunlight at the four riders in the distance.

"Who do you figure they are?" Ben asked, standing.

Tom made a wry smile. "Give you one guess."

"Devon."

"What does it mean, Uncle Ben?"

Ben grimaced. "It means your ordeal is about over, Andy, and Tom's and mine is about to begin." Ben limped to his saddle and came back drawing open his brass spyglass. He studied them a moment then passed the glass over to Tom. "It's Devon all right," Ben said.

Tom watched the riders through the glass and said, "Who are them others with him?"

"I don't know."

"May I see?"

"Here you go, chil'."

Andy put the spyglass to her eye. And then suddenly she was shouting, "It's my papa! It's my papa!"

Ben saw the worry that came to Tom's face. He was more terrified of Andy's father than he would have been of a dozen armed Neville Hallidaes. Ben put the spyglass away and came back carrying his Winchester. The riders were angling a bit too far to the north. Ben levered in a shell and fired into the air, and then a second shot. The riders down below drew up and changed their heading.

"Come on, Tom. We got a few minutes. They'll find Andy all right now."

Tom and Ben gathered up their horses. Ben paused a moment to consider the mule with its valuable cargo. "Leave it," Tom said, seeming to know what Ben was thinking.

Ben nodded his head and hunkered down by Andy. "Tom an' me, well, we got to be going. You understand why."

She did.

Ben gave her a smile. "I'm going to miss you, Andoreana."

Andoreana suddenly wrapped her arms around his neck and gave Ben a hug. She reached up for Tom and he lowered to her and got a hug too. "Please be careful," she said.

Tom had the book in his hand. "Here, Andy, you take it. I guess you and me won't be reading 'bout how Huck and Jim made out after all. I want you to have it. You tell your papa how old Ben and Tom here helped you out, okay?"

Andoreana took the book. "Thank you. I will."

Tom hesitated. "Andy, you wouldn't maybe tell that marshal that me an' Ben, well, maybe we lighted out o' here by, say, another direction, would you?"

Andoreana Dean looked at him, and Ben could see the struggle within the child. Finally she shook her head and said, "But that would be lying."

"Of course it would," Ben said sharply at Tom. "And I will not have Andoreana lying for us. You tell them whatever you have to," he said, stepping into his stirrup and swinging a leg over his saddle.

Andoreana was troubled.

Tom mounted up and gave the coming riders a long stare. "We only got a few minutes. Let's ride, Ben." He turned his horse away.

"Wait!"

They turned back. Andoreana seemed to have come to some decision. "Ride that way." She was pointing at a spire of rock that rose a mile or so off to the south.

"That will take us back down toward Pitkin," Ben said.

"Please," she went on with a sudden, burning verve. "Just go that way, only after a while circle back and then be on your way as fast as you can ride in a different direction. Please!"

Tom gave Ben a curious look.

Ben said to Andoreana, "I don't know exactly what you got in mind, but we'll do it." Ben wheeled his horse around and he and Tom put their heels to their animals and galloped away. And soon the trees closed in behind them, and they rode out of Andoreana Dean's life forever.

Twenty-nine

His horse hadn't come to a stop before Franklin Dean leaped off its back and smothered Andoreana into his arms. There were tears down both their faces, and then Franklin pushed his daughter out at arms' length and scrutinized the child for the slightest indication that she had suffered at the hands of her captors.

Devon heard him ask if she was hurt, but beyond that, the concerns of his job masked out the rest of it. He stepped wearily to the ground, and so did Landy. Hedstrom rode on beyond the clearing to study the land beyond. It had been a relentless pursuit, and now it was at an end. It hadn't come as Devon had suspected it might.

Three bodies twisted in death upon the grass of the mountain meadow. *A peaceful enough place to die,* he thought as he toed over the first body. Scott Mcintyre's jowly face looked back at him through eyes already clouded over. It didn't take long for death to steal away that indefinable glow; that quality present even in the eyes of the very sick. How quickly it flees once life has passed.

Devon hunkered down near to Turner Wilson, turned the man over, and frowned at the huge exit wound that had laid open his chest. He rolled him back onto the bloodied grass and strode to the third body.

Neville Hallidae. Devon had wanted to take Hallidae back alive to answer for his crimes in Judge Springer's court. Well, Hallidae was going to miss out on that judgment. Devon picked Hallidae's gun up out of the grass and slipped it over his finger where the other two guns dangled.

"Marshal." Landy came from the pack mule. "Whoever they were, they lighted out of here in a real big hurry. Left all the money behind still tied on back of that mule."

"Hallidae, Turner, and Mcintyre are the ones here. That makes it Tom Deveraux and Ben Masters who got away."

"It's funny, Marshal, but it almost seems they wanted us to find them."

"Not them, deputy — her." He nodded his head at Andoreana. "They wanted us to find the girl."

Hedstrom came in and reined to a stop. "Marshal, there's maybe a dozen riders coming up from the town below."

Devon grunted and nodded his head in reply. He walked back to Franklin Dean and his daughter. Franklin looked at him and said, "She isn't hurt."

"Pleased to hear that," he said, but his brain was already looking ahead to what needed to be done next.

Franklin noticed the doll in Andoreana's hand. "Where did you get that? We found Susie Meyers back along the trail."

"That mean Mr. Turner cut up Susie Meyers with his big knife. Then Uncle Ben bought me a new doll." Andoreana sighed. "But somehow, she just isn't the same as Susie Meyers."

"Uncle Ben?"

"Mr. Masters — only he said I could call him Uncle Ben. He took care of me when they found me after the fire."

"After the fire? You mean, the fire happened before they came to the house?"

Andoreana nodded, and looked sad.

"Then it was the stove, after all."

"No. Mama was very careful to make certain it was out before we went to bed, and to have a bucket of water."

"Then what happened?"

Emotion caught in her throat, and tears suddenly filled her eyes. "It was the lamp. Randy accidentally knocked it over, only the fire didn't start until we were all asleep. It must have been smoldering under the house."

Franklin took her into his arms again and held her tightly.

"I'd say you owe Ben Masters a bit of thanks for watching over your little one there, Dean," Devon said.

"And Mr. Deveraux, too," Andoreana said suddenly. "He kept that Mr. Wilson from hurting me. And he gave me this book."

"Are they among those dead, Marshal?"

Devon shook his head. "Those were the two that signaled us. They must have taken off right after." Devon gathered up the reins of his horse and lifted a tired leg over the saddle. He looked down at them and said, "There appears to be a posse on its way up from the town below. Judging by all this newsprint blowing in the wind around here, I'd say someone down there in Pitkin outsmarted Neville Hallidae, and now they are coming to finish the job. I'll be leaving you now."

Devon turned to Landy. "Saddle up, we still have two more to find."

Hedstrom rode over. "What about those men coming up?" And about that time the riders appeared on the edge of the meadow. Devon reined over and halted in front of the man who seemed in charge.

"Deputy United States Marshal Walter Devon," he said, thumbing back his vest to clearly show the badge. "You in charge here?"

"Sheriff Geckhorn," the man replied. "I'm in charge. What's a Deputy U.S. Marshal doing here in Colorado, anyway?"

Devon showed him the authorization paper signed by the governor.

"Ain't never heard of such a thing," Geckhorn said, returning the paper.

"Well, now you have. There are three bodies over there. I'm putting them in your charge. I'm also putting in your charge that man and his daughter. They've been through a little hell, sheriff; do what you can to help them get their lives back together. My deputies and I are going to follow the two remaining members of this here gang."

"You need some men, Marshal?"

Devon shook his head. "I don't think that will be necessary." He turned away from Geckhorn.

Back with Franklin and Andoreana Dean, Devon asked, "Did you have a rough time of it, Andoreana?"

She said, "I'm all right now."

"We will both be all right now, Marshal."

"Well, I need to keep on until I get them all. Andoreana, which way did Ben and Tom go?"

Andoreana seemed to hesitate, then she pointed at the spire of rock to the south. "Last I saw of them, they were riding off in that direction," she said.

Devon looked back at her. Something in the

way she had said it made him consider the child closer now. "You certain? That way takes them back down toward Pitkin."

Andoreana shrugged her shoulders. "That's the way I saw them go."

"Humm?" He glanced questioningly at Franklin.

"If Andoreana says that's the way they went, Marshal, that's the way for certain."

"Then that's the way we are going. Landy, gather up that mule. It's coming with us."

Geckhorn and his men were already collecting the bodies as Devon, Landy, and Stanley Hedstrom rode away toward the spire of rock Andoreana had pointed out. The sheriff moved about the open ground purposefully, giving directions to the men gathering up the bodies. He stopped by the mule to examine the packs and discovered that they were filled with money. Stolen money to be sure! Kathleen Hamil's money was here, among the rest, he realized all at once, and as he led the animal back to where his men were packing up the bodies, Harlan Geckhorn's thoughts were suddenly on the woman, and he was pretty certain she was thinking along the same lines as he.

Geckhorn seemed to stand a little taller now as he brought the mule over, and he was anxious to be back to town; anxious to see the look on Kathleen's face when he returned the money Neville Hallidae and his gang had taken from her.

"Well, don't that beat all."

"Let me see?"

Ben handed Tom his spyglass. They had made it to higher ground, now far north of the spire of rock, and Andoreana.

"She just couldn't tell a lie. Not to save our pitiful souls, she couldn't tell a lie. That's why she had us ride toward that rock. She sent Devon in the wrong direction!" Ben couldn't help but laugh aloud.

Tom watched them through the spyglass, then handed it back. "She's given us time, Ben. The kid did it after all."

Ben put the glass away. "Well, where to now?"

"Somewhere far away from here."

"I've been thinking about Missouri."

"I know you have."

"You want to ride along?"

The black man considered the offer, then shook his head. "I don't think so, Ben. Missouri is too much like Georgia. Hard for a black man to get a fair shake where he's so outnumbered." He grinned then. "Seems like a nigger can't keep himself out of trouble in white man's land."

"Then where?"

"Maybe I'll head down to Mexico. I hear that folks are more tolerant down Mexico way."

"Folks are folks wherever you go."

"Maybe so, but now that Andy's given me the chance, I want to give it a try."

"I'll see you again someday, Tom."

"I'll buy you a bottle of tequila when we do."

Ben grinned and reached out his hand. "Take care, then."

Tom grasped it, and for a long moment it was as if neither man wanted to let go. Then the moment passed. Tom reined his horse around and rode away to the west without looking back. Ben turned east. He suddenly had his family on his mind, and a country where green grass and wide forests grew, and a life he had left behind ten years ago. . . .

We hope you have enjoyed this Large Print book. Other Thorndike Press or Chivers Press Large Print books are available at your library or directly from the publishers. For more information about current and upcoming titles, please call or write, without obligation, to:

Thorndike Press
P.O. Box 159
Thorndike, Maine 04986
USA
Tel. (800) 223-6121
(207) 948-2962
(in Maine and Canada, call collect)

OR

Chivers Press Limited
Windsor Bridge Road
Bath BA2 3AX
England
Tel. (0225) 335336

All our Large Print titles are designed for easy reading, and all our books are made to last.